14/22

FREQUENCY

LISA HARRIS

Adrenaline-Fueled Fiction

DAY 350

CHAPTER ONE

DECEMBER 5TH

THE FEUD between the Gillards and the Wilders was legendary in Van Horn. Even before the grid went down, the two families had fought over everything from crops, to animals, to property lines, while regularly throwing out every accusation imaginable. Deputy Kellan Gray pulled slightly on the reins of his horse, Dante, as he headed toward the neighbors' adjoining properties with his partner, Deputy Miles Porter. The oldest of the Gillard boys had ridden into town, requesting help for an escalating conflict between the two men. *Whatever that meant.* This wasn't the first time law enforcement had stepped in to stop a fight.

Last month, Camden Gillard had insisted on a manhunt for the person who had stolen his prize rooster—and that person, of course, had to have been Hugo Wilder. The month before, Hugo had shot at his neighbor, claiming Camden was trying to kill him when his bees ended up on Hugo's property, and he allegedly almost went into anaphylactic shock.

Typically, the sheriff's department response was to ignore the two fools. As long as no one actually got hurt, Sheriff Estrada's position was to let the men battle it out on their own. The Quake, as some called it, had shifted the priorities of every lawman Kellan knew, shoving petty feuds even further to the bottom of the department's agenda. But today, a frantic visit from Camden Gillard's oldest had convinced the sheriff to send out a couple of deputies. Kellan and Miles had been given little information other than the fact that the two men were once again battling it out, and Gillard's son was terrified that this time the argument was going to end in bloodshed.

"What do you wanna bet that this time Camden sicced his bees on Hugo on purpose?" Miles asked.

"It's possible." Kellan adjusted his cowboy hat on his head to block the sun, then shrugged, uncommitted.

As far as he was concerned, he could deal with feuds like the Gillards and the Wilders as long as he was also doing something to make a difference in this town. The recent arrest of a string of traffickers resulting in the release of the girls they had taken captive had been one of those differences.

There was no way around the fact that the grid going down had changed everything. Not just for the small west Texas town he called home, but for the entire state and beyond. They still knew very little about who or what was behind the shutdown of the grid, or how widespread it was, but what little they had heard indicated it had hit the entire country. With bandits plaguing the roads, travel to major cities was difficult if not impossible. Any news that had trickled in—including a recent convoy sent from the Texas governor—had not been enough to give them any solid answers. So for the time being, they continued doing everything they could to keep Van Horn and the towns around them safe without any of the traditional modern resources law enforcement was used to.

Which wasn't easy, although Kellan had to remind himself that he could be living in far worse places. Too many of the towns he'd visited across the county with the sheriff no longer had any rule of law. They had been taken over by gangs, and some of their residents had simply disappeared.

This part of west Texas, different from anyplace he'd ever visited, was wild and remote, and he never tired of the incredible vistas. Around him was desert scrub and cactus that eventually gave way to forested mountains formed from volcanoes. He'd taken dozens of backpacking trips with friends. Followed trails dotted with white-tailed deer and breathtaking views. But anymore, he found little time to explore the surrounding terrain. Most of his time was spent like today—stopping feuds, dealing with thefts, and checking on people's well-being in the community.

"So. . . Who is she?"

Kellan glanced at Miles. "Who's who?"

"Seriously, Kellan. How long have we known each other? Your mind is a thousand miles away. And you've got that odd smile on your face. I just figured it has to be a girl."

Kellan frowned at the shift in the conversation. There was no girl. Not really. Though if he was honest with himself, there was someone he hadn't been able to put out of his mind. Not that he had any plans to pursue a relationship. Tess McQuaid lived a day's ride away by horse-back, and it wasn't like he could just pick up his cell phone and talk with her.

Still.

There was something about Tess. She was smart, resourceful, and not afraid to step outside her comfort zone. He'd seen it in the string of murders by the drug cartel. Her sketches had been a piece of the puzzle that helped them track down who was behind the grisly killings. He knew the task had been difficult, and yet she'd done what was necessary in this new reality of theirs. No electricity or labs meant no way for forensic evidence to be processed. Solar-powered chargers allowed them to have limited access to their phones, which meant they could take crime scene photos, but charging batteries took time, and at some point they would stop working. Having sketches was essential.

From their limited time together, he'd found Tess to be funny, smart, and undeniably beautiful. But this was not the world for a long-distance relationship. On top of that, his job was extremely demanding. When the grid went down, crime rose drastically. Everything from burglaries, to fights, to murder. Working under Sheriff Estrada's experience had been a plus, but the reality was being on call 24/7 with very little downtime. He wasn't even sure where a relationship could fit into his life.

"Am I right?" Miles pressed.

"All I'm thinking about right now is putting an end to this feud, getting home at a decent hour, and getting a good night's sleep."

"Nice way to shift the subject, but I'm still convinced you're thinking about someone."

Out of all the deputies the sheriff had hired, Miles was the easiest to work with. He didn't complain, didn't annoy him with corny jokes, and for the most part didn't pester him with personal questions.

Apparently today was an exception.

"And now I'm thinking by your lack of response there clearly is someone," Miles pressed as they turned onto the feuding neighbors' street.

"I might have met someone," Kellan said finally, knowing that the man was going to keep asking until he gave him something. "But she lives in Shadow Ridge."

"Does she have a name?"

Kellan paused again, really not wanting to go there. He knew Miles. He might be easygoing, but when he got his mind set on something, he could be more persistent than a swarm of bees.

"Tess McQuaid."

Miles grinned. "So, when you were in Shadow Ridge last month, you weren't just there on business?"

"Oh, I was there on business," Kellan said, immediately regretting that he'd mentioned her name. "Tess just happened to be part of that business."

"It sounds like I need to let the sheriff send me on some of those ventures."

"Not enough women for you here? Seems like every time I see you, you're with someone different."

"Ouch. I'm just. . .friendly. Unfortunately, with the limited options we have, I haven't found anyone who tugs on my heartstrings." Miles clicked his tongue to get his lagging horse to speed up. "But the McQuaids. They're legends. Does Garrett McQuaid know you're interested in his daughter?"

"No, and he never will. Because there's nothing going on between us and there won't ever be."

Kellan heard the shouting as they approached the adjoining properties. The two houses sat back from the gravel road, about fifty yards from each other. Clothes, strung on lines, flapped in the wind. A wooden fence had been built on the property line between the two houses years ago, but today it was full of holes and broken boards. But none of that had captured Kellan's attention.

Tied to a large oak tree in the middle of Hugo Wilder's front yard, was his neighbor, Camden Gillard. Hugo had a shotgun pointed at Camden while the men's wives argued on the sidelines.

"Out of all the possible scenarios, did this ever cross your mind?" Kellan asked, jumping down from his horse at the edge of the driveway and securing the reins to a post.

"Not exactly." Miles dismounted then set his hands on his hips. "How in the world are we supposed to deal with this?"

"That's a good question."

Kellan let out a huff of air as he strode toward the clashing neighbors. Out of everything he'd seen over the past year, *this* had to be the most ridiculous. In fact, if he had his way, he'd simply let them fight it out right here, right now, but obviously that wasn't going to work. Along with the wives, half a dozen children were watching the unfolding drama from inside the houses. If that didn't motivate the men to stop, Kellan didn't know what would.

Hugo stomped toward them. "What took you so long—"

"Hugo. . .I need you to put the gun down," Kellan said to the burly man. "This has gotten out of hand."

"You're exactly right," Hugo shouted. "He stole my chickens, that cantankerous fool. Ten of my Australorps are gone. You need to arrest him. Now."

"I didn't steal your chickens." Camden's bearded face reddened as he shouted back, trying unsuccessfully to pull himself free from the ropes. "You're the one who's gotta keep them pinned up. They're always coming over to my property and eating out of my garden."

Kellan held up his hands as he marched toward Hugo. "There are solutions to your problems, but you can't go around tying people to trees."

"What was I supposed to do until you got here? Y'all are as slow as molasses on a cold morning."

"Where exactly did you think he was going to go?" Kellan asked, his irritation rising. "Put your weapon down. Now!"

"What about my chickens—"

Kellan stepped forward, his hand on his holster. "Your children are watching what is going on out here. Watching what you're doing—"

"He *stole* my chickens—"

"Doesn't matter." Kellan signaled to Miles to take Hugo's gun. "I've had enough of this feud between the two of you. I'm arresting you both, right now for disturbing the peace, disorderly conduct, kidnapping—"

"Arresting me?" Hugo hesitated, then handed Miles his rifle. "I'm not the one who stole anything."

Kellan started counting under his breath in an attempt to keep his anger in check. *One. Two.* What kind of example were these men setting for their children?

Three. Four.

"You tied your neighbor to a tree and held him at

gunpoint." Kellan finally controlled himself enough to speak out loud. "I don't think any more explanation is needed."

"What about me?" Camden asked, still trying to tug free from the ropes. "I didn't kidnap anyone. I'm the victim here."

"My husband's right." Becky Gillard wiped her hands on the front of her apron as she walked toward him, her voice rising. "He didn't tie his neighbor to a tree."

Kellan ignored all of them as he went to untie Camden. The sheriff had told him to handle things as he saw fit, which was exactly what he was going to do.

"Here's what's going to happen," he said as soon as Camden was untied and both men cuffed. "The two of you are going to be spending some time in the same jail cell. Sharing a sink, toilet, and meals. And you will remain roommates until you put this feud behind you. I don't care if it's a day, a week, or a month."

"You can't do that," Hugo spouted. "We have rights."

"Last time I checked, I was the law around here. And if I want to put you in the same jail cell together, that's exactly what's going to happen."

"They'll. . .they'll kill each other." Becky's voice broke, the panic in her voice audible.

"Then maybe you better talk your husband into stopping this nonsense." Kellan motioned for the men to start walking, then turned back around to the wives. "And by the way, just so you know, we serve oatmeal for breakfast, soup for lunch, and stale bread and soup for dinner. So don't think this is going to be a vacation. If you two women want to supplement their meals, I don't have a problem with that."

"You can't do this—"

"Mrs. Gillard. . .Mrs. Wilder." Kellan set his hands on his hips. "I can understand that you too are frustrated, because I'm frustrated as well. But I've also had enough of this. My suggestion to both of you would be while your husbands sit in a jail cell, figure out a way to solve these problems just in case they don't. You've got children. Have them fix the fence. Repair the coop. Whatever it takes to stop this feud. We have an entire community struggling to survive, and every time I come out here, it takes me away from those who really need help. Those who are struggling to put food on their table. Struggling to raise animals. Struggling because they're lacking medication. Real problems."

Becky glanced at Hugo's wife then took a step back, clearly surprised with Kellan's candid response.

"I suspect it's gonna take a while before you can pick up your husbands," Kellan continued, "so until then, get things sorted out here. And pray they get things sorted out between them."

Kellan walked to his horse and mounted up before addressing the men. "The two of you will be walking. In front of us."

Hugo glared at him. "You can't do this. You can't treat us this way."

"You tied your neighbor to a tree. I don't think you have any room to talk."

They headed toward town at a slow pace with Hugo and Camden grumbling in front of them, but Kellan felt no sympathy toward them. All he could hope for right now was that a few days in the same jail cell would knock some sense into the two men.

Kellan heard the sound of horses behind him as they left the property. Two men riding hard came toward them. Kellan recognized them immediately once they got close enough to see their faces. Jacob Hahn and Abe Lynch.

Kellan pulled on the reins of his horse.

"Deputies. . ." Jacob said, stopping in front of them. "We were on our way to town to get help."

"What's going on?" Kellan asked.

"Abe and I were doing security out at the ranch and heard someone shout. A man's fallen into the old Cooper mine."

Kellan's jaw tensed at the news. Before the grid went down, federal agencies had worked across the state to close abandoned mines. But even though the entrance to the Cooper mine and others in the area had warning signs posted, they hadn't prevented several accidents over the past year alone from curious explorers. Some had ended in broken bones, but one man had lost his life. Deteriorating conditions over time caused the ground above the mines to become unstable, and there were gases and undetonated explosives that could easily escalate an already deadly situation.

"Do you know who he is?" Kellan asked.

Jacob shook his head. "He just said his name was Mac. I don't think he's from around here."

"What about his condition?"

"He's wedged under a wooden beam about six feet below the mine's opening where the ground gave way," Abe said. "We tried to get him out, but couldn't. And he's hurt pretty badly. Broken leg and a possible punctured lung. With extra men, we should be able to move the beam and pull him up."

Kellan glanced back toward town. If they took the time to go get help they'd add at a minimum of an extra thirty minutes. Given the dangers involved in this kind of accident and the man's injuries, they didn't have that kind of time.

With his options limited, Kellan didn't hesitate with his answer. "Hugo. . .Camden. . .I need the two of you to put aside your differences and come with us to the mine to help get this man out."

The men looked at each other, clearly not thrilled with the idea, but they both nodded.

One of their sons still stood on the edge of their property. Kellan quickly shouted at the boy to bring their horses.

Kellan dismounted in order to uncuff the men, then stepped in front of them. "So help me, if either of you cause me any trouble, I'll make sure you're still in the jail cell over Christmas."

After giving instructions for the boy to go to town and get Dr. Alfaro, the men mounted up and the group headed toward the ranch in silence. They all knew how high the stakes were. The limited medical resources they had after the grid went down often escalated simple accidents into life-threatening events. If they were dealing with something like a punctured lung, he wasn't sure that his EMT training was going to be enough to save the man. And delayed treatment could lead to the rapid deterioration of the patient because of his inability to receive the oxygen his body required.

FIFTEEN MINUTES LATER, the men approached the mine where the ground had given way at the base of a large rock formation. There was an abandoned horse grazing to their left that Kellan assumed belonged to their victim. Beyond the mine were open grasslands with the silhouettes of mountains in the distance.

He studied the situation before stepping forward, knowing that the unstable setting made it just as dangerous for the rescue team as the victim. From his limited vantage point, he could see that a large wooden beam sticking out of the mine entrance had shifted and in the process trapped the man who'd fallen inside.

"I'm going to talk to him while the rest of you try and dislodge that beam that's pinning him down," Kellan said. "Go slow. We can't have the mine collapse on top of him."

The man would be buried alive, and they could go down with him.

Kellan made his way carefully to the opening of the partially collapsed mine shaft, then lay down on his stomach and flipped on his flashlight. He could see the man lying ten feet below him and the beam that was crushing his leg.

"Mac?"

The man's eyes fluttered open. Good. At least he was still alive.

"Mac, my name is Kellan Gray. I'm a deputy and here to help. Can you tell me what you're feeling while my men try to get you out?"

"I don't know. . ." He closed his eyes again.

"Mac. . .I need you to stay awake and talk to me."

The men had moved into position, but so far the beam hadn't budged.

"I'm not sure how much longer I'm going to last. My leg is broken..." The man gasped for air. "It's getting. . .it's getting hard to breathe."

"I've got five men up here working to get you out, and then we'll deal with your medical issues. I just need you to hang in there."

His flashlight caught blood covering the man's shoulder with what looked like a bullet wound. "What happened to your shoulder?"

"I. . .I was shot."

Kellan looked up at the makeshift team, grateful that Hugo and Camden were working together, but the men were still struggling to make any progress. And now he'd just learned their victim had been shot.

"Who shot you?" Kellan asked.

"I don't know." The man turned his head. "You. . .you said you were a deputy?"

"Yes."

"If I don't make it. . .I—I need to tell you something."

"You're going to make it—" Kellan countered.

"You don't understand." The man closed his eyes for a moment, his chest barely moving with each breath. "I'm with the FBI. Three of us were heading to Austin with a flash drive full of information for the governor, but we. . .we were ambushed a few miles back. Lawrence. . .he was shot. And Manning. . .I don't know where he is. I think they took him alive. The men in the security detail we were traveling with are all dead."

"That's when you were shot?" Kellan asked.

"Yes."

A wave a nausea swept through Kellan. "Where did this happen?"

"West of here. I managed to get away and ride this far. Something spooked the horse, I was thrown off, then. . .then fell into the shaft."

Kellan worked to process the information as the man continued.

"It's a matter of national security. I have information about what's going on that has to get to Austin. News about . . .about the grid going down, and the people behind it. They've hired bandits. . .thugs. . .making communication almost impossible."

Kellan's mind spun. He'd heard dozens of conspiracy theories as to what had taken down the grid. China, environmental activists, aliens. . .If this man had answers, he needed to find out everything the man knew.

"Do you know how widespread the shutdown is?" Kellan asked.

"They've hit the whole country plus Canada. . .Mexico. . . We're still trying to confirm how widespread it is beyond our borders. All. . .in. . .in an attempt to take over. . . cause confusion."

"What's their end game?" Kellan asked, trying to stop the terror growing in the pit of his stomach.

"Don't know. Yet. It's an. . .an underground group. Multi-national. Cyberattack shut down satellites. Jammed signals. . .hit the electric grid, internet, water networks, and transportation. . . They call—"

Mac started coughing.

The beam slipped another inch.

One of the men shouted.

"Mac?" Kellan called out.

"They call themselves. . ." He coughed again, and blood

trickled down the side of his mouth. "They call themselves The Realm."

CHAPTER TWO

A YEAR AGO, Tess McQuaid had been studying the history of fine art, design theory, and composition in Austin. Today she was trying to help her sister, Dr. Hope McQuaid, keep a four-year-old from having a meltdown after shoving a button up his nose.

"Peter, I really need you to stay still." Hope let out a frustrated breath as the little boy flung himself against his mother, crying as if he were being tortured.

Tess caught the frustration in her sister's voice and turned to Peter's mother. "Mrs. Michaels, maybe it would be easier on both you and Peter if you just stepped outside for a moment. He'll be fine. I promise."

Mrs. Michaels hesitated at the suggestion before thrusting Peter into Tess's arms and stepping out of the room. Peter sucked in another breath, ready to scream again, then stopped as soon as the door shut.

Tess bounced the boy in her arms and flashed him a smile. "Do you know what happened when I was little and got a raisin stuck in my nose?"

The question shifted Peter's concentration for the moment. He shook his head.

"I got a lollipop as soon as it was taken out," Tess said.

Peter's eyes widened. "Really?"

Tess nodded.

"Do I get a lollipop?" Peter asked.

"If it's okay with your mother, *but*. . .before the lollipop, I had to sit still and let the doctor take it out."

Hope nodded at Tess to continue, obviously relieved.

Tears had left tracks on Peter's face. "Did it hurt?"

Tess grabbed the flashlight Hope had out on the table, turned it on, and shined it on Peter's belly. "Does that hurt?"

Peter shook his head.

"All my sister needs is a flashlight and these tweezers. That button should pop right out."

"Ready?" Hope asked.

Peter hesitated again and then nodded. Five seconds later, the button was in the boy's hand and Tess was off to find a lollipop.

"You know you're the perfect assistant," Hope said, giving Tess a hug once Peter and his mother had left. "I'm just not sure what's going to happen when we run out of lollipops."

"Compared to some of the things I've had to stomach, this was nothing," Tess said, wiping down the exam room with a DIY disinfectant spray. "Even if I could go back to school, I definitely wouldn't switch to the medical field."

Hope glanced up from the folder where she was updating Peter's file. "You miss school, though, don't you?"

"I try not to think about it. I just get. . ." Tess shrugged as she finished disinfecting the room, searching for the right word. "Frustrated, I guess. Sad."

"That's completely understandable."

She'd loved her first semester away from Shadow Ridge. Her classes had challenged her, but they'd also confirmed she'd picked the right major. Thanks to the Quake, though, she'd only finished one semester of art school. But while there were plenty of days when she would do anything to go back in time, she'd finally had to accept that going back to normal wasn't going to happen. At least not anytime soon.

The front bell of the clinic rang, signaling another patient.

"It doesn't ever end, does it?" Hope headed toward the door.

"Not when you're the only clinic around," Tess said. "But you look tired. When's the last time you took some time off?"

Hope stopped in the doorway of the exam room. "How am I supposed to take a day off?"

"I don't know. Maybe you need to delegate more," Tess said, putting the disinfectant back under the cabinet. "You don't have to be the one pulling buttons out of a four-year-old's nose."

"I know, it's just that. . ." Hope's gaze dropped to the tiled floor. "Staying busy is good for me."

"Maybe, but wearing yourself out isn't." Tess caught the sadness in her sister's gaze. "You miss him, don't you?"

Hope blinked back the tears and nodded. "I know I'm not the only one whose plans changed after the Quake, and I have a lot to be grateful for, but Chase. . .I have no idea where he is, or even if he's alive." She shook her head.

"My heart knows that he would do everything he could to come back to Shadow Ridge. Back to me. But he hasn't. . ."

"He will." Tess reached out and squeezed her sister's hand. "Somehow I just know both Chase and Sam are out there and will make it home."

Hope had reconnected with her college boyfriend, Chase Beckett, right before the Quake. The weekend the grid went down—the weekend of their parents' fortieth anniversary—he'd been transferring prisoners to Midland. Two of her three brothers, Jace and Levi, had made it to Shadow Ridge for the anniversary party, but her other brother Sam and Chase didn't make it back. They hadn't heard from either of them for almost a year. All they could do was pray that one day they would all be back in Shadow Ridge eating around the table together once again for the weekly McQuaid family dinner.

The reminders still felt raw, because there was one McQuaid who was never coming back. Their mother had died the day of the Quake in a car wreck. There were still days when Tess woke up wanting to run downstairs and talk to her mother. And then reality would hit her. Her mother was not coming back. At least they still had hope that Chase and Sam would return.

Her father had been even more affected by the loss of Katherine McQuaid, and in some ways she felt as if she'd lost both of her parents that day. Her father had taken a bullet while out on a fugitive hunt, and the combined loss of his wife, his health, and his job as chief of police had led him to a place where he'd given up.

Over the last few months, he'd made some changes. He was riding again and taking Ranger, his police-trained

German shepherd, with him. But for the most part, her father still kept to himself. If it wasn't for Margaret, she wasn't sure what they would have done. The older woman, who'd been friends with her parents for years, had moved into the ranch house and taken over the running of the house and the therapy of her father. She had become like a second mom to Tess and had managed to make more progress with her father than anyone.

But some days the losses were too overwhelming to deal with.

A knock on the exam room doorframe pulled Tess from her thoughts.

"Hope, I'm sorry to bother you, but Frank just walked in with his wife." Karen glanced down at her hands. "You're not going to like this, but the skin on her arm is red, and she's had some nausea, muscle cramps, and diarrhea."

Tess glanced at her sister and caught the panic in her eyes. She didn't have to say anything because Tess knew what Hope was thinking. This wasn't the first time someone had come in with these symptoms. And three days ago, they'd buried two more of them.

"Tess, I need you to go to the police station and get Jace," Hope said.

"You think it might be the same diagnosis?" Karen asked.

"I don't know," Hope said. "But if it is, we're looking at a potentially devastating community health crisis."

TEN MINUTES LATER, Tess was headed back to the clinic with her oldest brother. Jace was former military intelligence who had stepped up as the law in town after the Quake, along with their brother Levi, who'd graduated from the police academy. The aftereffects of the grid going down had dictated the need to bring on additional part-time officers, but Tess knew that the small police force still found themselves stretched thin, without any outside resources for the secluded, west Texas town.

"I saw Morgan yesterday," Tess said as they crossed to the other side of Main Street that was lined with a number of undrivable cars. "I couldn't help but wonder why she still doesn't have a ring on her finger."

"Wow, sis. You're becoming direct."

Tess laughed. "You've been bringing her and Noah to our family dinners on Sunday. I figure you're wanting to make the relationship permanent."

Tess stopped on the sidewalk in front of The Book Nook. Like many of the empty shops that had once been the heart of the town, the book and art supply store had been boarded up since the Quake. "I also happen to know you've talked to everyone in the family except me about mom's ring."

"I have." Jace shoved his hands into his pockets. "I was planning to talk to you. I just. . .things have been extra hectic."

"I think it's more that you're worried it would upset me."

Jace hesitated. "You're the most sentimental of all of us, and I just. . .you're right, I didn't want to upset you—"

"I think using mom's engagement ring to propose is a wonderful idea," she said.

"You do?"

They started walking toward the clinic again. "Of course. I think Morgan's perfect for you."

Jace's smile widened. "I don't know what I was expecting, but thank you."

"One thing I've been reminded of over the past year is that family—and those we surround ourselves with—matter far more than things."

"Agreed, though you're the one in the family who refused to let mom throw away that paper mâché pig you made. It sat on the top of the fridge for years."

"I was also six."

"Touché."

She nudged her brother with her shoulder. "I just want you to be happy, and Morgan clearly makes you happy."

Hope was standing at the front desk of the clinic when they arrived and quickly motioned them back to her office.

"I saw Judith Ramsey earlier this morning, and just now Frank and Kerrie. They all have the same symptoms I've been watching for," Hope said, getting straight to the point.

She shut the door behind her, then sat down at her desk.

"How many?" Jace stopped in front of the window, his hands behind his back, while Tess took a seat across from her sister.

"So far I've had nineteen come in with the same red and swollen skin and gastrointestinal issues. I've been able to manage most of their symptoms and have come up with a protocol, but with three dead, I'm very worried. Whatever we're dealing with, it's definitely spreading."

"What's your best theory?" Jace asked.

"I was up half the night doing research." She glanced at her cluttered desk covered with books and handwritten notes. "All of my research points to arsenic exposure. I have no way to accurately test, but the symptoms match."

"Where is it coming from?" Familiar feelings of fear surfaced as Tess posed the question.

With no running water, most people had come up with a catchment system that enabled them to harvest rainwater. It was one of the many things they'd had to do in order to survive, but it clearly held risks if that was the source of the contamination.

"Tainted drinking water, leaks in water wells. . .It would definitely explain all of this." Jace took off his cowboy hat and tapped it on Hope's desk. "Tell me, how do we deal with this?"

"We need to find the source. I know there are hundreds of thousands of abandoned oil and gas wells across the country. West Texas definitely has its share of abandoned wells, and even if we're not using them, it is possible for the poison to leak into the ground and contaminate it. It was an issue before the Quake, but dealing with the health problems of the pollution now is going to be even more challenging."

"Why would wells be leaking arsenic?" Tess asked.

"The locations of many of the abandoned wells aren't even documented," Jace said. "Which means a lot of times symptoms can develop without people knowing the source, and when these contaminates get into the water supply, it can bring on headaches, digestive issues, and all kinds of other health problems. "

"Can we go in and plug them?" Tess asked.

"There are ways to look for them," Hope said. "In the

past, states actually hired well hunters. They use metal detectors, grounded air surveys, and sometimes even drones, but obviously we can't do that."

"The town won't make it without water," Jace said. "So what are our options if your theory is correct?"

"We've been looking into ways to purify water, including prickly pear," Hope said. "The results are actually very good. Tess knows more than I do. She's been helping set up the test filters."

"Ava and Josie found several journals that belonged to their father," Tess said. "Some of the stuff in there is actually pretty amazing. Everything from making salves, to healing herbs, to water purification systems. That's where the prickly pear comes in."

"Prickly pear gel?" Jace asked, sitting down in the empty chair next to Tess.

"I've already been using it as a poultice," Hope said, "and it can be rubbed onto the skin for burns and abrasions."

Jace leaned forward. "How does it purify the water?"

Hope nodded at Tess to answer.

"The gel can collect clusters of bacteria pathogens," Tess explained, "and in theory should filter out almost a hundred percent of the microbes. Using Ava's father's notes, we've come up with a prototype filter system that uses the prickly pear gel to strain the water. So far, no one who has been using the filter has gotten sick."

"I'm assuming they didn't teach you that in art school, but I'm impressed," Jace said. "Do we have any idea how widespread this is?"

Hope picked up a pen and tapped her desk. "Part of the problem is that I have no way to accurately test the water to confirm the presence of arsenic, leaving potentially dozens if not hundreds of people out there with life-threatening situations."

"And in the meantime? How are you treating patients?" Jace asked.

"We're treating the symptoms, which are anything from vomiting, to dehydration, to cardiac issues. Beyond that, I've been doing research on therapeutic measures to counter the poisoning."

"And. . .," Jace prodded.

"I found a study in one of my medical books about a combined treatment program of spirulina extract and zinc. I started the treatment with two of my patients who are suffering from what I believe to be the arsenic poisoning."

"Are you seeing any results?"

"I've noted some lessoning of symptoms, but no therapy will be effective in stopping the symptoms from developing if we can't stop the exposure to the poison."

"So we need to find the source of the outbreak, but also set up as many water filtration systems as possible," Jace said.

Hope nodded. "Exactly. In medical school, we studied how epidemiologists search for the cause of a disease when an outbreak occurs. I've already started mapping out the limited information I have, so hopefully, we will be able to identify a pattern and a source."

"And thus prevent more outbreaks," Tess added.

Hope dropped her pen back onto the desk and leaned forward. "But we're going to need to inform people about the situation. Even without cell phones, news spreads rapidly, and if people hear about the outbreak. . ."

"They're going to panic," Jace finished for her.

"They've already started," Hope said.

"I'll meet with the mayor and set up a town meeting for tomorrow, but I'll need you to be prepared to address the situation."

Hope nodded. "Of course."

"I need to get back to the ranch," Tess said, standing up. "I promised Margaret I'd help her with dinner."

Jace's frown conveyed a reminder that he wasn't thrilled with her riding back and forth to the ranch alone. "Be careful."

"I have my sidearm," she said, touching the gun on her hip that her father had taught her to use. "I'll be fine."

"I might be delayed," Jace said, "but I'm planning to be there for dinner. I need to talk to Dad about a few things."

"Like Morgan and an upcoming engagement?" Tess prodded.

"I'll see you later tonight, Tess," Jace said, ignoring her question. "And please. . .be careful."

Tess left the clinic, then headed out of town on Sugar, her horse that had replaced the Hyundai Kona she'd been saving for. Jace wasn't the only one in her family concerned about her insisting on riding to and from town on her own. Part of her determination was simply due to the difficulties it would cause if she required an escort every time she needed to go to town. The other part was that she needed a sense of freedom in a world where so much had been taken away.

Something about riding that had always made her feel free. And now it was the one place she could almost forget everything that was going on around her. She'd grown up riding horses, and that feeling had never lost its magic. With the desert and distant mountains surrounding her, the ride from town to her family ranch never failed to give her a sense of solitude and freedom.

But sometimes the solitude felt overwhelming. Everyday brought so much to worry about. So many *what ifs*. She understood Hope's need to stay busy, because she felt the same way. The more time she had to think, the more time it gave her to worry.

She started past the neighbor's place, then stopped at the yappy bark of a dog. Walter Phelps's Scottish terrier had somehow gotten loose, and her collar had gotten snagged on something near the front gate.

Tess pulled slightly on Sugar's reins, then quickly dismounted. "Hang on, girl. I'm coming."

Walter lived on the land next to the McQuaid ranch, a large piece of forested property with mountainous views to the west. Tess had started stopping by on her way into town a couple times a week after discovering that the old man was lonely. Folks in town avoided him because he was known to be cantankerous, but it didn't take long for her to realize that the man had a sense of humor and was a wealth of information.

"What are you doing out here, Prim, and where's Walter?" Tess asked, as she worked to unhook the dog's collar from a low-lying tree branch.

Prim had belonged to Walter's wife. He was a retired show dog she'd loved to show off until her death three years ago. And while Walter had never claimed to even like the dog, Tess knew for a fact that he would be heartbroken if anything happened to her. Which was why it was strange to see her alone this far from the house.

Tess walked to the house with Sugar on one side and Prim on the other, surprised when there was still no sign of Walter. The older man spent most of his time outside tending to his garden, where he was currently growing collard greens, brussels sprouts, turnips, and beets, among other cold-tolerant vegetables. Despite his grumpy front, Walter always managed to give away far more food than he kept.

"Walter? Walter, are you here?" Tess set Prim down beside her as she stepped up to the front of the house and knocked on the door. "Walter?"

Nothing.

Prim started back up with her yappy bark as Tess tried the door. The handle turned, so she stepped inside, calling once more for Walter. She found him lying on the yellowed-linoleum floor of the kitchen, his body already stiff from rigor mortis, his eyes partially open, and a red rash on his arms.

CHAPTER THREE

TESS WANTED TO RUN, but she couldn't move. All she could see was Walter's stiff body, lying in the middle of the kitchen. It wasn't the first dead body she'd seen. The Quake had brought with it a number of tough situations she'd been forced to deal with. Things she'd never imagined herself being capable of doing. The first crime scene she'd gone to, she made sketches for the police records. Jeremiah Daniels had been murdered by a gang so they could steal what was in the town warehouse and resell it on the black market. The last crime scene she'd sketched had been of a girl not much younger than her, who'd been taken by a group of traffickers and killed when she tried to escape.

Tess's fingers clenched at her sides until her nails bit into her palms. There were no outward signs of trauma on Walter's body. Just the familiar red rash that she'd seen on the others at the clinic.

She looked around the small kitchen with its peeling paint and worn countertops. She tried to think back to

when she'd last been here. Three...maybe four days ago?
Hope had talked about the symptoms of the poisoning.
Weakness...nausea...headache...difficulty   breathing...
Walter hadn't mentioned any of those things. She knew
enough from listening to Hope that the severity of the
reaction depended on the amount of the toxin ingested
and length of exposure.

How had he died so quickly?

Prim ran past Tess toward Walter. Tess quickly scooped
the dog up. She couldn't stay. She was going to have to find
one of her brothers. Because if anyone found out that
Walter was dead, she knew what would happen. There
were those who would descend on the property like
vultures, fighting over everything he had left behind.

She glanced at the curio cabinet filled with Walter's
wife's collectibles and the family photos hanging in a row
on the wall next to the dining room table. Those keepsakes might not be worth anything in today's world, but
as a former marine, Walter had survival equipment stored
in this house that was worth plenty on the black market.
She wasn't going to let thugs come in and destroy what
he'd worked so hard to build over the past two decades on
this land. Pushing back the swell of emotion pressing
against her throat, she took one last look at her friend,
then hurried back outside toward Sugar with Prim in her
arms.

Prim managed to stay still in her lap as Tess rode to
the family ranch surrounded by open savannahs, rolling
hills, and distant mountains. The sun was already begin-
ning to slip closer to the horizon, and in another hour the
day would be met with the shadows of night. She considered going back into town, but the ranch was closer, and

she knew Jace was planning to stop by later this evening. Besides, she always avoided traveling alone after dark.

Ten minutes later, Tess made her way up the long drive toward the two-story house with its covered veranda and red barn that had been owned by her family for five generations. In the past, the ranch had raised grass-fed steers, but the Quake had forced them to scale back their production of cattle, chickens, and other livestock. Several of the ranch-hand wives had started a community garden where they grew produce not only to feed the families who lived on the property, but to trade the excess for other essentials or give it away to those in need.

Margaret, who had spent the last year caring for her father after he was shot, sat on the porch peeling potatoes.

Tess jumped down off Sugar while still holding Prim, secured the horse, and headed for the house.

"I'm not sure your father's going to want to take on another animal," Margaret said, smiling as Prim jumped up into her lap and started nuzzling against her.

"I was planning to try and find her a home."

"Whose dog is this?"

Tess frowned. "Walter Phelps."

"Walter? I knew she looked familiar. Maggie used to take her to shows to compete all the time."

Ranger, her father's German shepherd, ran out of the house onto the veranda, sniffed Prim, then went to Tess. Apparently, he was uninterested in their temporary guest.

Tess knelt down to scratch Ranger's head while the smile on Margaret's face faded.

"Where is Walter?"

Tess let out a huff of air. She didn't want to say it out loud, as if telling Margaret Walter was dead would somehow make it real. She wanted to think she'd somehow made a mistake. Somehow imagined what she'd seen. A glance at Prim reminded her that she hadn't imagined any of this.

Tess swallowed hard and stood back up. "Walter's dead."

"Dead? How?"

"I don't know, but I think he died of the same thing the Palmers died from."

Margaret's face paled. "Which is?"

"Hope's not sure, but she thinks it might be arsenic poisoning from the water."

Margaret set the dog down, stood up, and started pacing. "Ugh. If it's not one thing it's another. Raiders coming through the town, girls being stolen, and now arsenic poisoning. . ."

"I need to talk to Jace or Levi. I know at least Jace is supposed to come tonight, but I could head back and try to find them—"

"You know how your father feels about your being out after dark, and that includes your brothers. It's not safe, and I'm afraid you wouldn't get back in time."

"I know." Tess's hand went automatically to the slim gun in her holster. "I feel like I'm living back in the Wild West. I've somehow gone from carrying a backpack full of textbooks to a handgun."

Margaret shook her head. "I think we all feel that way."

Tess glanced at the open front door. "What about Dad? Is he awake?"

"He put in quite a workout today. He's lying down until dinner."

Tess nodded. "I'll finish changing, and then come and help you."

She started into the house, then stopped and gave Margaret a hug.

"Are you okay?" Margaret asked.

"Yes." Tess blinked back the tears. "I was just reminded today—again—of how fragile life is."

Tess picked up Prim, grabbed a candle from the entryway table for when the sun went down, then headed upstairs to her bedroom. Streams of yellow light flowed through the open window, leaving a soft glow on the wooden floor. She sat down on the quilt her grandmother had made and felt the surge of emotion she'd been trying to hold back since discovering Walter's body.

No one could escape loss in this world, but the last year seemed to have amplified its reach. It seemed unfair that Walter had lost his wife and now had died alone in his house. Unfair that her mother wasn't here to help her navigate this new world.

"Tess?"

"Dad. . .Hey."

Her father walked into her room and sat down on the edge of the bed. Even though he'd made progress with his physical therapy, his limp was still pronounced. Garrett McQuaid was a man who'd always seemed bigger than life to her. A man she'd adored as a little girl, and one she still looked up to. He'd cherished her mother and loved each one of his kids. Ranger ran into the room behind him, again ignoring Prim, who'd curled up on Tess's bed, and lay down next to her father.

"Margaret just told me what happened. I'm so sorry you had to find Walter."

"Me too." She drew her knees to her chest and wrapped her arms around them, knowing she'd never be able to unsee Walter's lifeless body. "I hate how death and tragedy have become so much a part of life. Sometimes I feel like we're balancing on the edge of a cliff just waiting for the next piece of bad news to drop."

Her father reached out and squeezed her hand. "Tell me about it."

"I found him on my way home."

"Do you have any idea what happened to him?"

"Maybe." Tess shrugged. "Hope will have to confirm, but there was a rash on his arm. I think it could have been arsenic poisoning, the same thing that killed the Palmers and Mrs. Sullivan."

Her father rubbed the back of his neck. "The water."

"Yes. Hope has no way to actually test the water, but that's her theory. I told you how Josie and I have been using her father's journals as a resource for a water purification system, but I'm scared." Tess pulled Prim closer to her. "If there is arsenic in the water system, this will affect all of us."

"And more people are going to die," her father said.

Tess nodded. "And what's worse, Walter was using the filtering system. If it really worked, like we thought it did, Walter would still be alive."

"And I haven't helped." Her father reached out and squeezed her hand. "I've been needing to apologize to you."

Tess turned toward her father, giving him her full attention. "What do you mean?"

"Losing your mother took away a big part of me, but I'm realizing that I'm not the only one who suffered from her loss. You lost your mother. And I... I haven't been there for you the way I should have."

"You lost more than just the love of your life. You lost your career, your health... I've missed you, but I don't resent you." Tess shook her head and moved to sit closer to him on the edge of the bed.

He kissed the top of her head, then pulled her against him. "So much has changed. I guess I'm still trying to find my place in all of this."

"We'll always need you. You're the glue that holds this family together."

"No, your mother was the one who held this family together. I haven't been there for you, Hope, or your brothers, and that bothers me. You've seen and had to deal with so much. It's not something you've talked about with me, but Jace keeps me informed. He told me about the crime sketches you've done. And now Walter?"

Tess blinked quickly and looked away. He was right that so much had changed. And that in reality nothing would ever be the same. "It hasn't been easy. But knowing that I'm helping... That makes me be able to do it."

"I just worry about you. You're supposed to be in college with your whole life ahead of you, but you're here, stuck in Shadow Ridge, glassing eggs with Margaret, helping me with therapy, and working with patients at the clinic. I want you to know that what you do is noticed. And appreciated."

"Thank you." She leaned her head against his shoulder. "There are some advantages to all of this. I'm here with you, Hope, Jace, and Levi, and a lot of my friends."

Her father looked away, but she didn't miss the flicker of pain in his eyes, knowing he was thinking about Sam, who never made it home last December. Life and loss had become so closely tied together, and yet she was constantly reminded that there never had been any guarantees. They were only actually guaranteed the moment they were in.

"This has been difficult, and yet you've risen to the occasion," her father said. "You haven't let things knock you off your feet. Only God knows the future, but so far you've managed to play a pretty significant role in Shadow Ridge."

She frowned, unsure she deserved the compliment. "Most of the time, I stay busy so I don't have to think. I miss Mom, Sam, and just being a college student. I miss the chance of learning and friends and maybe getting married one day. It feels like so much has been put on hold."

"I wish I had an answer to all that. The Quake changed everything, I know that. I just. . . I just wish I could fix things."

"Well, it's not the first time I've wished we could go back in time." Tess smiled. "Sometimes I lie in bed and convince myself that when I open my eyes everything will be back to the way it used to be."

"You're not the only one. But in all my years, there is one thing I've learned that has helped ease the pain. Life is full of seasons. Some are good, and some not so good. And the interesting thing is that usually the not-so-good ones are when I've found the most growth." Her father reached down to pet Ranger, who'd stood up next to him. "Though I'll confess this has thrown me and challenged me in ways I don't like to admit. But I'm trying. I just want you to know that."

She wrapped her arms around his neck. "You'll always be enough for me, and I'll always be your little girl, no matter what."

"Until you finally find that man of your dreams."

"In Shadow Ridge?" Tess laughed as she scooted back on the bed and pulled her knees up to her chest. "Somehow I don't think that's going to happen."

"What about Gideon Savage? I've been impressed with him."

"He's nice, but nice isn't enough." She shifted, feeling awkward about discussing boys and romance with her father. She was looking for someone who challenged her, but also someone who stirred something inside.

Like Kellan Gray.

The thought took her by surprise. They'd met a few weeks ago, when he'd been in Shadow Ridge helping with a case. At the time, she'd decided to ignore the attraction she felt toward him. He had shown no interest in her, and even if he had, he lived in another town. She had no idea when she'd see him again, and that wasn't the kind of relationship she wanted. Besides, getting to know each other long distance wasn't exactly a possibility in the world they lived in.

"What are you thinking?" her father asked.

She stood up and kissed him on the cheek. "That I'm hungry and I need to go help Margaret with dinner."

Tess pushed aside thoughts of Kellan, his gorgeous eyes and broad shoulders, as she headed downstairs. She'd have to leave the handsome deputy in the category of fairy tale. Because she'd learned firsthand that not all stories in this world ended happily ever after.

CHAPTER FOUR

KELLAN PACED INSIDE the lobby of the clinic that was located a few blocks northeast of the sheriff's department, waiting for news on the man they'd managed to pull out of the collapsed mine. Dr. Alfaro was one of three doctors caring for not only an entire town, but a number of surrounding small towns in the county. With no electricity and limited resources, running the clinic had become one of the town's biggest challenges.

Kellan had seen the shape Mac was in, and he was pretty sure he wouldn't make it. Which was frustrating. If the man had information about who was behind the grid going down, they needed to know.

Kellan glanced up as Sheriff Estrada stepped into the lobby, dressed in his uniform. He had been the sheriff in this county for the past five years and had become the backbone of the community, thanks to his out-of-the-box thinking, especially after the grid went down.

"I came as quickly as I heard," the sheriff said, sliding

his sunglasses into his front shirt pocket. "What's going on?"

"The man we found is injured pretty badly and is in with Dr. Alfaro right now," Kellan said. "Long story short, he claims he's with the FBI and that he was one of three agents heading to Austin with information for the governor. They were traveling with a security team, but they were ambushed a few miles away."

The sheriff pulled off his cowboy hat, wiped the back of his neck with a handkerchief, then set his hat back on his balding head. "I need you to tell me everything he said."

"I don't know much," Kellan said. "He doesn't know where the other two agents are. He said one was shot, and his security detail is dead."

"What information were they carrying?" Estrada asked.

Kellan glanced across the lobby, thankful it was quiet here this afternoon with only half a dozen people waiting to see the doctor and no one sitting close enough to overhear their conversation. Until they knew more, this information needed to stay confidential.

Still, Kellan lowered his voice. "Information about the grid going down. I don't have details, just that one of them was carrying a flash drive with information on who's behind it. He said they've hired bandits and thugs to keep things stirred up, which is part of the reason we've found communication to be almost impossible."

The sheriff frowned, deepening the creases across his weathered face. "What else?"

"According to Mac, the man we found, the Quake hit the whole country plus Canada and Mexico. And I guess they're still trying to confirm how widespread beyond our borders, but they believe it's sabotage."

"What's their end game?" the sheriff asked. "Whoever's behind this."

"I'm not sure how much the FBI knows. He mentioned a multi-national underground group with cyberattacks that shut down satellites and in turn have affected the electric grid, the internet, water networks, transportation. . ." Kellan paused, trying to stop the terror growing in the pit of his stomach. "He said they call themselves The Realm."

"*The Realm?*" The sheriff leaned forward. "What is that?"

"You now know everything I do," Kellan said. "I'm assuming he has more information, but the doctor doesn't want anyone asking him questions right now. Sounds like he's in and out of consciousness."

"We need the information that man has." The sheriff started pacing in front of Kellan and rubbing the back of his neck, as if trying to come up with a solution to an impossible situation. "We don't know who's behind this. We don't know their end game. We don't know what The Realm is. Or what information they were carrying." He froze. "What about the flash drive?"

"I've gone through his possessions several times, but no, I couldn't find anything. There were some food rations, but nothing official. Not even a badge."

The sheriff dropped his hands to his sides, frowning again. "Then how can we know he's even telling the truth?"

"I'm sure he's telling the truth," Kellan said.

"You can't know that."

"The man was dying, and he was terrified," Kellan said, trying to explain what his gut told him. "Whatever message he needed to get to the capital was valuable. Valuable enough to kill for."

"I have to say, it does make sense." Estrada sat down on one of the empty chairs behind him and leaned forward. "You mentioned a cyberattack. Over the past few years, there's been a growing race to put satellites in the air, and as a result some of the cybersecurity standards are subpar. And if they were hacked, it could cause havoc to the infrastructure, transportation, electric grid, and water."

"Which is exactly what we've seen." Kellan sat down next to him on another green-padded chair. "The problem is, we don't know where these guys are or what message they were trying to get through."

The sheriff rested his arms on his thighs, the fatigue Kellan knew he felt reflecting in his eyes. "I want to say it sounds like some big conspiracy theory, but the fact that I can't turn on a light or a faucet makes me believe you're right."

"I guess in the back of my mind I always hoped that all of this was some mechanical breakdown, like a meteor strike or a major earthquake. That there weren't people behind the destruction."

"Something tells me that if that were true, it wouldn't be so widespread and we'd have far more information by now. Instead, it really feels like someone doesn't want us to know what's going on."

At this point, there was no way to know, but if some group like The Realm was behind all of this, they were going to need to move quickly and get as much information as they could.

"Mac said that their security team was dead, but there's the possibility that the other two agents are still alive. We need to find them," Kellan said.

"Agreed, but they could be anywhere, and we don't even know who we're looking for. We need to talk to this Mac guy."

Kellan stood up. "Then we need to talk to Dr. Alfaro."

Kellan followed the sheriff past reception to find the doctor. Before the grid crashed, long-term critical care patients were stabilized in the adjoining hospital, then transferred to El Paso. Now, due to limited resources, only the clinic was available to treat patients.

They found the doctor wearing scrubs and talking to one of the nurses.

"Afternoon, Dr. Alfaro."

"Sheriff." The doctor handed the clipboard he'd been holding to the nurse. "What can I do for you?"

"The man my deputy brought here," the sheriff said, getting directly to the point. "We need to talk with him."

"He's got a punctured lung, a gunshot wound, and has lost a lot of blood. He's awake, but honestly, I don't expect him to make it."

The sheriff glanced at Kellan for a moment, then made his decision. "We need to talk to him."

"I would highly advise against that—"

"And in most situations I would follow your advice, Doctor, but this is urgent. And you know me. I wouldn't ask if I had any other option."

The doctor hesitated, then nodded before signaling

them to follow him to the patient's room. "Just keep your time with him short."

Dr. Alfaro hadn't been exaggerating. The man looked as if he'd been in a street fight, and his face had paled to a pasty white.

The sheriff shut the door behind them, then stopped at the edge of the bed. "I'm Sheriff Estrada. My deputy is the one who found you."

Mac tried to move to his side but winced in pain. "What happened?"

"Don't move, please. You're here at the clinic in Van Horn."

"I can't stay here," the man groaned.

The sheriff stepped forward. "I know you're in a lot of pain, but we need to talk. You mentioned The Realm to my deputy. I need to know everything you can tell me."

Kellan stood on the other side of the bed, his hands clasped behind him while he prayed silently that Mac would stay conscious long enough to give them the information they needed. They'd learned so little as to why the grid had gone down. Knowing they were so close to finding another piece of the puzzle made getting the man to talk vital.

"I don't know. Everything is so fuzzy."

"You were shot," the sheriff said. "And I'll be honest, it doesn't look good. If you have information that needs to get somewhere, this is your chance."

"The information I have is highly sensitive."

The sheriff sat down on the edge of the bed. "You told my deputy here that the information you had was a matter of life and death. I don't know what needs to be done, but I can promise you that we will do everything we can to get that information where it needs to go. We just need to know what it is."

Mac squeezed his eyes shut. "There's a flash drive."

"Where is it?"

Mac hesitated, as if he were searching his memories, but from the heaving of his chest as he struggled to breathe, Kellan knew he didn't have much time.

"One of the other agents was carrying it. Lawrence Haley. On it are names. . .names of those involved in The Realm. Those determined to destroy this country. Intel pointing to where their base of operations is and other classified information. We need that intel."

"Do you have any idea where Agent Haley might be?" Kellan asked. "Any at all?"

Mac's hands trembled. "Haley had it stashed on him. We were attacked. Shot. I don't know where he or our third agent, Aaron Manning, are. We were traveling undercover. No badges in case we got caught."

"Can you give me a description of the missing agents and the route you were taking?" The sheriff pulled a notepad out of his pocket.

"White. Males. Both about six feet. Haley has a sleeve tattoo. Right arm. American flag." Mac reached up and grabbed the sheriff's arm. "Please. You need to find them. On that flash drive is a list of undercover agents who have infiltrated The Realm in an attempt to stop their efforts. If that list of names gets out, those men are dead. And without that information on The Realm, we're going to be helpless. . .helpless to stop them."

Kellan took a step forward. "There's the possibility that you were simply attacked by one of the gangs that have formed since the Quake."

"Maybe," Mac said. "If that's true, they probably don't know what they have. But imagine the worth of that file on the black market if they were to find out. You've got to find Haley and Manning and make sure the drive gets to the capital."

Sweat beaded across Mac's forehead. His chest heaved as if he couldn't get enough air.

"I'm sorry. . . I. . ."

"I'm going to get the doctor," Kellan said.

He opened the door and signaled for Dr. Alfaro. "He's struggling to breathe."

The doctor rushed into the room, putting an end to the conversation. "I'm going to need you both to leave. I'm sorry."

"Just keep us updated," the sheriff said as they headed out into the hallway.

Kellan followed the sheriff into the lobby, then outside to where a cold wind was blowing across an empty parking lot.

"They can't be that far away," Kellan said.

"I can send out four of our deputies. We can alert neighboring law enforcement to send out search parties. Maybe we'll have a slim chance of finding them."

"I'll go," Kellan volunteered.

He knew that riding alone was dangerous, but he'd rather it be him out there than one of the married deputies. Besides, resources were already stretched thin.

The sheriff nodded as they strode to their horses. "I'm going back to the office for a while, but I want you to go home and get some rest. I want you to head to Shadow Ridge first thing in the morning, and let the McQuaid brothers know what's going on. See if anybody has any

information. Somebody might have seen or heard something. If we can pick up their trail and track them down,
we might be able to find that flash drive."

"Garrett McQuaid's the best tracker in the county,"
Kellan said mounting his horse.

"If he's willing."

"He was involved in finding those kidnapped girls not
long ago."

Kellan understood the sheriff's hesitation. Shadow
Ridge's chief of police had walked away from law enforcement after being shot by a fugitive. That, and the loss of
his wife, had understandably shattered the man's world.
Still. . .from everything he knew about him, Garrett
McQuaid was a man you wanted on your team in situations like this.

The sheriff turned to Kellan from the saddle of his
palomino. "Before you go. . . Just be careful out there.
You've become an invaluable member of our team. I don't
want you to think your hard work has gone unnoticed."

"I appreciate that, sir," Kellan said.

"Stop by the house on your way out of town in the
morning. I'll make sure my wife has enough food to get
you to Shadow Ridge."

The sun was already setting when Kellan arrived at the
small, detached room behind Sheriff Estrada's house. He
wasn't used to having a father figure. Or at least one that
treated him decently. In his mind, fathers left, and were
typically out of the picture.

He glanced up at the cross hanging on the side of the
sheriff's house. Kellan believed in God. Believed He was
the Creator of the universe. Even believed He'd sent His
Son to die for him. But seeing Him as a heavenly Father

who cared about him as a son. . .that wasn't something he'd ever been able to understand.

He shook away the doubts as he took care of his horse, then went inside his room. He needed to get some sleep, because tomorrow was going to be a long day.

CHAPTER FIVE

"SNICKERS!"

Tess had forgotten about Walter's cat. She threw back the covers and jumped out of bed before heading for her closet in the semidarkness of morning. She pulled on a pair of jeans and a shirt, then fumbled in a drawer for a band to pull her hair back into a ponytail.

For the most part, Walter had tended to stay to himself, especially the older he got, but his daughter had given him a cat several years ago while visiting from back east. Snickers, who acted more like a dog than a cat, had become his constant companion.

She grabbed her boots then headed downstairs to the kitchen where Margaret was heating a pot of coffee on the wood stove. No matter how early she got up, Margaret was always already in the kitchen planning, canning, or glassing eggs, along with a long to-do list necessary to keep food on the table.

"Tess?" Margaret turned around as Tess charged into the kitchen. "What's going on?"

Tess grabbed the pair of boots she'd left beside the open kitchen door. "I'll be back in an hour to take care of the chickens, but I've got to go find Snickers."

Margaret cocked her head. "Snickers?"

"Walter Phelps's cat. She's there by herself with nothing to eat, and after seeing Walter. . . Well, I totally forgot about her yesterday."

Margaret glanced next to the wood stove where Prim lay curled up in a ball on an old towel. "You know the last thing we need is another stray animal."

Tess bit her lip. "I know, but I can't let her go hungry."

Margaret grabbed a mason jar off the shelf. "I may or may not have taken in several stray cats before I came here."

Tess grinned as she pulled on the boots, knowing she'd never have to convince Margaret—or her father for that matter—when it came to taking in strays.

"Want to at least have some breakfast?" Margaret asked, turning back to the stove. "I don't think your father is going to want you to go out there by yourself, and he's out with Ranger. There's no telling who's going to show up who shouldn't."

A seed of fear sprouted in Tess's gut. She knew what Margaret was hinting at. Six months ago, the town had voted about what happened when someone passed away and there was no family or relatives to take over the estate. The voting procedure had gotten ugly a few times, but eventually a protocol was put into place. If someone died without any local heirs, the property and its contents were to be divided and given out to those in need. The house itself would then become available to those on a list who needed housing.

"I promise I'll be careful," Tess said. "I'll find the cat, then come straight back here."

Tess finished tying her boots, then hesitated before slipping her handgun into her holster. Her father had taught her how to shoot, but she'd never imagined having to carry the lightweight Glock 43 every time she went out. Prayed she never had to use it to defend herself.

"Take this for the cat." Margaret handed her the mason jar that was now filled with fresh milk. "And please. . .be careful."

The sun was just coming up over the horizon as Tess started toward Walter's. While so much had changed, the desert remained a constant that had helped her to find joy in the small things. The smell of rain, the blue skies that went on forever, and the scattering of brush and cactus that would turn into colorful flowering spots in the spring.

Along with the beauty, though, she'd seen her share of tragedy and death. Walter Phelps was just one of those whose death had affected her on a personal level. His house came into view. Her last visit with him had been strange. He'd been unusually agitated. Even for Walter Phelps. He'd started talking about his daughter. About regrets. About things he'd wished he'd handled differently.

Michael Koonce, one of the newer volunteer officers for the police department, stepped around from the back-side of Walter's house as she arrived.

"It's just me Michael. Tess McQuaid."

"Morning." Michael pulled off his hat and slapped at a bug that had landed on his pants.

"Is everything okay here?" she asked.

"Been quiet all night, thankfully. They've taken the body, and now I'm just waiting for my replacement."

"Who is it?"

"Gideon. He should be here any minute. I need to head home and help Beth with the animals."

"Why don't you go on home?" Tess secured Sugar at a post on the side of the house, then walked toward the porch. "I'm sure he'll be here soon. I'm just gonna find the cat, then leave."

"Are you okay?" Michael settled his hat back on his head, then hesitated. "I heard you're the one who found Walter's body."

"I was." Tess bit back the sadness. "I should have come by sooner. I didn't even know he'd been sick—"

"You know it's not your fault."

A part of her knew that, but true or not, it didn't make her feel any better. "Have you seen Walter's cat?"

"Nope, but it could be hiding in the house. There are dozens of good hiding places with all that stuff of Walter's."

"He's a bit of a packrat."

Was a bit of a packrat.

Tess flinched at the reminder that Walter was dead. She stared at the peeling paint

on the outside of the stucco house. Like so many others, Walter was another person who would be alive if not for the Quake.

Like her mother.

Anger flared in the pit of her stomach. The combination of the overwhelming grief that went hand in hand with loss fought to pull her back into a dangerous emotional downward spiral she knew all too well. The only thing that had kept her moving forward this past year was family and not giving herself time to think. And her faith.

She'd talked to her pastor about her struggling faith as she tried to justify in her mind why God allowed so much suffering, hurt, and loss. She knew the question had no easy answer and that suffering didn't mean the absence of God's presence. But holding on to that truth was easier some days than others.

"You sure you don't mind if I leave?" Michael's question brought her back to the present.

"No." Her hand went automatically to her sidearm. "I'll be fine. There's a good chance the news of Walter's death hasn't even gotten out yet, and besides, Gideon will be here soon."

Tess stepped into the house as Michael rode away. The musty smell of dust mingled with smoke from the fireplace. While Walter had been a bit of a grouchy old man, he'd always lit up when she came to visit. But now... Now he was gone.

She walked through the living room toward the kitchen, looking for the cat.

"Snickers? You in here? I've got fresh milk. I know you're hungry, and probably scared."

The dining room was full of papers and stacks of magazines and books alongside vintage records that could no longer be played. But there was no sign of Snickers. She stopped next to the table where Walter had started a puzzle—a photograph of the New York City skyline. Besides some of his survival stash, there was little of value in this place. Just memories of an old man, like the curio cabinet filled with keepsakes his deceased wife had left him.

Tess called the cat again, then picked up a pocket-sized notebook from the end of the kitchen countertop. She'd seen it before, usually in Walter's shirt pocket, but he'd never told her what it was. She hesitated for a moment, then opened it up. Inside were doodles, scribbled notes, and dates. Walter had recorded the daily weather, what he had eaten for breakfast, lunch, and dinner, and books he had read. She stopped, smiling when she saw her name in a list of people who'd come to visit.

She continued thumbing through the pages, then stopped at a large *X* that had been underlined twice next to the letters *AS*. Right below were the letters *JP and RP*, and then the word *cover-up* was circled.

Tess glanced over the page again, then quickly closed the notebook, feeling suddenly as if she'd just glimpsed something she shouldn't have. Something personal. And yet what would happen to all of Walter's personal things? Food and clothing would be given to the churches to distribute. Then, if needed, the house would be taken over by someone who needed a place to live, like the Fergusons, whose house had burned down two weeks ago.

While the system worked, it still bothered her. She slipped the notebook into her back pocket, then turned to a family picture on the dining room wall of Walter and his wife and their girls taken at least a decade ago. As far as she knew, both daughters now lived somewhere on the East Coast. Walter had talked about them from time to time, but even he wasn't sure where they'd been when the Quake had struck.

Forcing herself to stay focused, Tess opened up the back door and started calling Snickers again, not sure what to do if she couldn't find her. Like Michael had said, there were dozens of places where a scared cat could hide inside the house.

When Snickers didn't appear after a couple minutes, Tess headed back inside. In the corner of the kitchen she noticed that the trashcan had tipped over, probably Snickers searching for something to eat. Tess grabbed a broom and dustpan from behind the door and swept up the mess. She started dumping the trash into the trashcan, then stopped, stumbling backward at the sight of a dead mouse on the counter. Apparently Snickers wasn't the only one hungry. Also on the counter was a plate of leftover chicken and potatoes from what must have been Walter's last meal. Was that what had killed the mouse?

She leaned the broom against the counter, done with the cleanup. With no way to refrigerate, food poisoning was always a possibility. A few months ago, an older man from town had died from what Hope believed to be salmonella. It was possible that salmonella poisoning killed both Walter and the mouse, but still, something didn't add up. Tess had seen the tell-tale patchy skin on Walter's arms that had marked the other victims Hope believed had been poisoned from arsenic in the ground water.

Walter, though, had been one of the people they'd set up with a filter that they were hoping would remove both iron and arsenic from the water. The system was made from two plastic drums with a sand-gravel mixture in the bottom to extract the clean water. So far, no one with the filters had shown signs of arsenic poisoning.

No one until Walter.

A sound shifted her attention outside. She glanced out the window and saw someone riding up to the house. She couldn't tell who the rider was, but it definitely wasn't Gideon's horse. She set her hand on her sidearm, questioning now her decision to let Michael go before his replacement arrived.

Tess stepped onto the porch, then let out a sigh of relief at the familiar face. "Mayor Shannon. . . I was hoping you were Gideon. He's supposed to be here any minute for his shift."

The mayor slid off of his horse, then tied it near hers on the side of the house. "I'm actually meeting Jace here. We need to come up with a plan to talk to the town. Not only do we need to get Walter's estate settled before someone breaks in, but people are scared. We're going to have to plan a town meeting."

"He told me that the two of you were going to meet."

Mayor Shannon came around to the front of the porch, then wiped his muddy boots on the doormat and stepped past her. "I'm surprised to see you here alone."

Tess shrugged. "Walter was a neighbor. A friend. And I'm the one who found him. Then this morning, I realized I'd forgotten about Snickers."

"Snickers?" the mayor asked.

"Walter's cat."

"Did you find it?"

"No, but I did find a dead mouse on the kitchen counter."

"Hmm. . . I know your sister believes that the recent string of illnesses are tied to tainted water."

Tess followed him into the kitchen. "That's her theory right now. Arsenic in the water. Except Walter was using a filter."

He started looking around the kitchen, stopping in front of the dead mouse. "I know you've been working on a filtration system, but being unable to test the water makes it impossible to know for sure how well it's working."

"True." Tess hated to admit it, but she knew he was right.

"Even with the filter, poison in the water system could still have killed Walter. And the mouse for that matter. If we lose our water supply. . ."

He didn't have to finish his sentence. Without water, Shadow Ridge wouldn't survive.

"Someone's out front," the mayor said, turning around. "Must be your brother or Gideon."

She started after him, but he held up his hand.

"Hold on Tess. . ." The mayor pulled out his sidearm. "I need you to get down. Now."

She froze at the unexpected command. "What? Why?"

"Someone's out front, but it isn't your brother or Gideon."

She hesitated, then crouched down next to the kitchen cabinets before pulling out her own gun. Looking up, she saw the tail of the dead mouse hanging over the side of the cabinet. A shiver slid down her spine.

"Who is it?" she asked, unable to see from her position.

"I don't know. A couple of armed men. And they don't look like they're here for afternoon tea."

"They're here to rob the place," Tess said. Clearly, news really did spread just as fast without cell phones.

The mayor nodded. "That's exactly what I was thinking."

"What do we do?" she asked.

"Stay where you are. I'm gong to see if I can get a better look at them."

The mayor slipped out of the kitchen. A second later, a gunshot ripped through the house, shattering the window in the adjoining room.

"Mayor. . ." Tess whispered.

He came back around the corner and grabbed her hand, pulling her to her feet. "We need to get out of here. Now. They must have seen me, because they shot out the window. Our only chance is through the back door."

She looked back toward the living room, catching a glimpse of the shattered window as he hurried her to the door.

"Tess. . .just do what I say, and you'll be fine."

She nodded. Maybe her father had a right to worry. If she hadn't come out here on her own. . .

She flew down the stairs behind the mayor toward the side of the house where she'd tied up her horse.

"Don't slow down," he ordered as they mounted their horses. "Don't look back. Just ride as fast as you can."

Ride as fast as you can.

Enough had happened over the past few months for her to realize that she had no desire to clash with whoever was about to come into that house.

Tess leaned forward, urging Sugar to speed up. Any moment, she expected a bullet to rip through her. Horse hooves thundered beneath her. The wind whipped at her face, but for now she was alive.

She had no idea how long they rode. Time seemed to have slowed down, making seconds feel like minutes. Her heart was still pounding from fear when the mayor finally slowed down and stopped among a small grove of trees.

"We need to give our horses a rest," he said, sliding off his saddle.

"Do you think they followed us?" she asked.

"It's possible."

Tess looked around, realizing for the first time that she had no idea where they were. They'd started out heading south from Walter's place, adjacent to her family's ranch, but they must have veered west. She could still see the familiar Davis mountains looming in the distance, but beyond that. . .

"Do you know where we are?" Tess dismounted from her horse.

"We can't be that far from town, though I'm not sure, exactly."

Tess frowned. The last thing she needed was to get lost out here.

"We need to get back to town," she said.

The problem was, even if they did make it to Shadow Ridge so she could let her brothers know what had happened, whoever had been at Walter's house was going to be long gone. It wasn't as if they could call 911 for help, or the sheriff for backup. And if Gideon or Jace had shown up, they could be outgunned and possibly ambushed.

"Did you hear that?"

She turned around. "Hear what?"

The mayor looked frightened. "Someone's out there. *They're* out there."

"You think they followed us?"

She could see movement in the distance, but couldn't tell who was coming. They were standing on the edge of a grove of trees, but finding a place to hide wasn't going to be easy. To their right was a small outcropping of rocks. They might be able to hide there, but they wouldn't be able to hide their horses.

Tess hesitated. "What if it's my brother?"

"Maybe it is, but we can't take any chances." He grabbed his horse's lead. "We need to head for the rocks and pray they don't see us."

She couldn't argue with him. She'd seen firsthand what some of these gangs were willing to do. Not blinking twice at murder was one of them. She led Sugar through the trees toward the rocks, praying with each step that they were making the right decision. Praying that her brother and the others were okay.

Tess felt a sharp prick in her neck as she stumbled over a fallen branch, then everything went dark.

CHAPTER SIX

KELLAN PRESSED his knees into the sides of his horse, trying to pick up the pace. Riding to Shadow Ridge today had not been on his agenda. Finding a man who had information on the grid going down had been just as unexpected. Tracking down the men responsible for Mac Hanna's death was going to be difficult. But the sheriff was right. If what Mac had said before he'd died ten minutes later was true, finding that flash drive was a crucial piece to ending this war.

He'd never thought of the grid going down as war, but that's exactly what Mac had implied. A group of traitors with an agenda that had brought with it complete chaos and upheaval.

His mind shifted for a moment to Tess. Before the Quake, as some called it, he'd been ready to find a wife and settle down. He never should've told Miles her name because his partner was right. Tess was the kind of woman he once had wanted to pursue, but the world had completely changed. While most of his friends had left west Texas as soon as they'd graduated, he'd decided to stick around. Not forever, but long enough to get some experience under his belt before relocating to a bigger city. Now he wasn't sure that time would ever come.

Barely a month ago, he'd investigated the murders of three young girls alongside the McQuaid brothers, and in the process had discovered drug runners not only trafficking drugs and black-market goods, but girls. Something that had been going on long before the Quake, but without communication and resources, discovering those behind the trafficking had been difficult.

Granted, everything had changed since the grid went down. There was little access to goods, no delivery services, no communications, and no internet service. Everything electronic had gone down, which meant no refrigerators, cell phones, air conditioners, or computers. Some of the cars still ran, but after a year, finding gasoline had become almost impossible. The first few months had been the worst. When the hospital's generators finally went out, people died. There wasn't enough law enforcement to cover the amount of ground they normally covered, and no backup available.

Law enforcement had always been challenging in rural West Texas. The county sheriff's office had always been used as support for police departments, many of which only had one or two officers. But now, with no way to communicate, law enforcement was no longer able to rely on the county sheriff's department. A difficult situation before the Quake now seemed impossible.

Many of the towns had brought on extra officers as a necessity, but it was difficult when there was no town budget. Communities ended up paying them with food from their gardens and fields. But there were also towns that had been left with no municipal departments, no troopers, and no dispatchers.

One of the answers Sheriff Estrada had come up with was to spend more time going from town to town throughout the county, making sure that information was passed on, as well as sharing resources between departments. Kellan had been assigned Shadow Ridge, where Garrett McQuaid had once been the chief of police.

The sheriff had done his best to give his deputies time off at least once a week, but the list of things that had to be done just to ensure there was food on tables and enough clean water was a full-time job in itself. Courting Garrett McQuaid's daughter on top of all these changes wasn't really an option.

Kellan kept riding, determined to put Tess McQuaid out of his mind. Maybe one day when all this was over he'd have a chance to find out if what he felt toward her was reciprocated, but for now, he was going to Shadow Ridge for business and nothing else. The stakes were far too high to allow a distraction.

For starters, they needed to come up with a way to find Mac's partners—assuming they were both still alive. Needed to ensure that the flash drive didn't get into the wrong hands. The problem was, how? How did they organize a manhunt when they couldn't efficiently communicate with nearby towns? Their pony express system of getting information to nearby communities had helped, but it wasn't going to be enough.

Movement up ahead shifted Kellan's focus and pulled him out of his thoughts. A saddled horse stood grazing in a small meadow next to a grove of trees. Which was odd.

Horses were highly valued animals, considering they were the best mode of transportation now.

He rode up to the horse and dismounted so he could look around. The horse's owner had to be nearby. But why was someone out here in the first place? Most people knew it wasn't safe to travel alone, let alone this far off the main roads.

He saw her as soon as he turned around. She was sitting on the ground, leaning against a large rock.

"Tess?"

She looked up at him, her dark eyes wide with confusion. "What happened?"

"That's what I'm trying to figure out." Kellan crouched down in front of her, looking for injuries, but finding none.

She rubbed the back of her neck. "Who are you?"

"Kellan Gray. We've met. In Shadow Ridge. I'm a deputy from Van Horn."

"Do you have a badge?" She shook her head as if she were trying to pull up the memories. "Because you're too young to be a deputy."

"Tess. . .Tess, I need you to look at me." He raised her chin slightly, trying to get her to focus on him. "Have you been drinking, or. . .I don't know. . .taking drugs?"

"Are you serious?" She threw her head back and let out a snort.

"Very." He pressed his fingers against her carotid artery in order to check her pulse. "You have all the symptoms of being drunk. . .or drugged."

Tess's smile quickly faded. "How is that possible?"

"I don't know, but your pupils are dilated, your heart rate is rapid—"

"With what? Because I don't take drugs. It's not possible."

He shifted his weight to his back leg. At least he had her attention now. "That's what I'm trying to figure out," he repeated. "Do you remember anything?"

"I was at the house," she said.

"What house?"

"Mmm. . .Walter's house. He lives alone on the ranch next to ours." She looked around, the confusion back in her eyes. "Where are we?"

"We're still a good distance from Shadow Ridge."

"How did I get here?"

Kellan bit back his frustration. They were going in circles. "That's what you need to help me with. Tell me about Walter."

Tess blinked, then shook her head as if she were trying to dig up memories. "He's dead."

"Dead?" Kellan frowned. Was her being out here somehow related to the man's death? "I need you to tell me what happened to Walter."

"I found him dead. I think it was arsenic poisoning. The water filter he was using didn't work."

"Makes sense," he said, trying to follow the logic of her story. "We've had the same issue in Van Horn."

But how did someone's death from poisoning connect with Tess McQuaid being drugged and left out here? So far her story wasn't adding up.

"What happened at the house?" he pressed.

She closed her eyes for a moment. "I went back to find Walter's cat. Snickers. I was worried about him."

"Okay. What else?"

"I spoke to the guard. Michael. We always have guards

in place until arrangements have been made with the family so thieves don't steal everything."

Something buzzed in his ear. Kellan turned, then quickly swatted away the grasshopper that had landed on his shoulder. "What else do you remember?"

"I told the guard he could leave. That I would be fine."

He studied her face. Her breathing had slowed some, and she was sounding more coherent, but he still didn't have the information he needed.

"Did someone else come to Walter's house?" he asked.

"Someone else. . ." She pressed her lips together, then gasped as if she'd just made some important discovery. "Mayor Shannon. He said he was meeting my brother Jace. He wanted to know what was going on because people were worried. He's planning to hold a town meeting and try to reassure them that everything possible is being done to keep everyone safe."

"Did anyone else come?"

"Maybe? I don't know. Everything seems fuzzy."

"It's okay. Just try to think."

"Someone else did come," she said, her eyes lighting up again at the memory. "The mayor heard someone in the front of the house, then there was a gunshot. The window shattered. He told me we had to get out."

"You're doing great, Tess. What happened next?"

"We ran. Got on our horses, and then . . .I don't know." This time the confusion in her eyes was replaced with fear as she reached for the empty holster on her hip. "There were gunshots. . .I blacked out. . .and not only is my sidearm gone, but I don't know what happened to the mayor."

"Don't worry." Kellan pulled his water bottle from his

bag and gave her a sip. "You're safe now, and your memories will come back."

At least he hoped they would. In the meantime, he wasn't sure what he should do. There was no way she could ride to Shadow Ridge on her own horse. She was still way too loopy.

She leaned toward him and shot him a smile. "Have I ever told you that you're cute?"

He pulled back, caught off guard. "I'm sorry?"

She reached up and ran her finger across his jawline. "Cute. Not like Snickers. Handsome."

He took her hand and moved it away from his face, unsure of how to respond. She'd definitely been drugged. This was not the Tess he knew.

"Tess, I need to get you back to Shadow Ridge. Your family is going to be worried."

"I wanted to ride back, but I was so tired, so I took a nap."

He could sense the intensity in her voice. He had no idea how long she'd been out here, but it was already afternoon, and if they didn't get moving, it was going to start getting dark.

"Maybe if I just took another nap—"

"There's no time for a nap." He stood up. "I'm going to help you stand up. Do you think you can walk around a little? That might help you wake up."

"Why can't I sleep?"

"Just trust me, Tess. Please."

She shrugged, then let him pull her up. At least for the moment she wasn't fighting him, but he had no idea how he was going to get her back to Shadow Ridge. Two adults riding a horse that distance wasn't the best idea, but waiting until she was more coherent wasn't necessarily a good idea either. He didn't like the idea of being out here once the sun set, and if they didn't get moving soon, that's what would happen.

He caught her loopy grin again as she leaned back against the large rock. At least he could think of worse scenarios than being stuck in the desert with a beautiful woman.

He dismissed the thought. She'd definitely been drugged with some kind of benzo. He'd dealt with victims before when he was an EMT, and the symptoms fit. He knew her enough to be confident that she wouldn't have done this on purpose. At least he didn't think so. But why would someone drug her? That's what he didn't understand.

She started to slide down the rock, but he pulled her back up against him. She needed to walk around and get the drug out of her system.

"I feel so tired. I really want to sleep." She rested her head against his chest. "Please."

"Tess, I know you're tired. It's because you've been drugged. But we need to get you home." He grasped her shoulders and held her at arm's length. "I want you to try walking around. Can you do that?"

Kellan wrapped his arm around her waist, not giving her time to say no, as they started walking through the trees. While she stumbled next to him, he tried to sort through his limited options. As long as she hadn't been overdosed, she should be okay. Treatment depended on symptoms, which could be as invasive as pumping the stomach, or simply observing. Depending on the amount that was in her, the effects should disappear within the next few hours. But they didn't have a few hours to simply wait it out. He needed to get her back to Shadow Ridge now, before dark.

Her hand trembled as she reached up to push her hair out of her eyes and then adjusted her knit beanie. "I must look like a mess."

"Not at all," he said. "I think you look. . ."

Perfect.

Kellan stopped himself from finishing the sentence out loud. No. Despite his partner's prodding, he had no intentions of trying to instigate a relationship with Tess McQuaid. They needed to stay on topic, and that meant figuring out what was going on.

"Tess. . .I need you to focus. Did anyone hurt you? Or maybe give you something to drink?"

She stopped next to him. "Something pinched me. It hurt."

Kellan grasped her shoulders again. Maybe they were finally getting somewhere. "Where, Tess? Where did it hurt?"

"My neck."

This scenario fit. If someone had drugged her with a syringe. . .

"Can I look?" he asked.

She pushed back her hair, then turned her head to the side.

It was there. A tiny, red mark.

"Someone drugged me?" she asked.

"Yeah."

She grabbed his hand. "Kellan. . .I'm scared."

"You're going to be fine, I promise. The drug will wear off, and I'm going to get you home."

"Thank you." The hint of a smile was back. "And I do trust you."

The strong desire to get to know the woman standing in front of him returned. Apparently putting Tess McQuaid out of his mind wasn't going to be possible. At least not for now.

Gunshots fired from a distance yanked him out of the moment. He pulled her down with him. Clearly, whoever had shot at her and drugged her wasn't finished.

CHAPTER SEVEN

TESS DROPPED to the ground next to Kellan at the sound of the gunshot, still trying desperately to clear her head. Nothing made sense. Memories still felt fuzzy, and everything around her felt surreal. As if she were watching from the sidelines. And yet that wasn't true. Someone had shot at Walter's house. She'd ridden away with Mayor Shannon, terrified she'd be struck by a bullet. But then what had happened?

Her hand went to her neck where Kellan had found the prick mark. She had felt something, but why had someone drugged her? And why was someone shooting at them now?

"Tess. . ." Kellan gripped her shoulder. "We need to get to the horses. We're outgunned, and I can't afford to waste my bullets by returning fire."

Two more rapid-fire shots exploded, and she watched in horror as her horse reared, then took off across the open field into another row of trees. A second later,

Kellan's horse ran off in the same direction. Tess tried to focus her mind, but couldn't. Surely this wasn't connected with what had happened at Walter's place, but she didn't know anything other than the fact that Walter was dead, the mayor was missing, and someone was shooting at her again.

"Tess." Kellan's grip on her shoulder tightened, pulling her away from her thoughts. "We need to get out of here. Now."

She didn't argue as he slid on his backpack, then pulled her up onto her feet toward the thicket of oak trees behind them. She had no idea which direction they were going. No idea which way led back to Shadow Ridge. And no idea how they were going to get there without horses.

"Do you know which way it is to Shadow Ridge?" she asked as she stumbled through the dense undergrowth beside him.

"Yes, but our shooters are blocking the direction we need to go."

She tried to listen for whoever had shot at them and who might now be following them, but all she could hear was their own feet trampling the dry layer of undergrowth. Still fighting the fog that had entrapped her mind, she struggled to keep up with Kellan. How could she have forgotten him? Those blue eyes, a hint of a beard adding a layer of ruggedness, and his smile. . . She'd memorized the lines of his face, the sound of his voice, plus hadn't missed how he looked at her the last time she'd seen him in Shadow Ridge. Or the stir of emotions he'd brought up in her.

She stumbled over a small branch, snapping it in half.

Her ankle twisted as she tried to catch her balance. Immediately, Kellan had his arm around her waist, ensuring that she didn't fall.

"Are you okay?" he whispered, giving her a moment to catch her breath.

"Besides the fact that I was drugged and now somebody is shooting at us?"

They stood still for a moment, his arm still tightly around her waist, listening for any movement behind them. The sun had already begun its descent toward the mountains, lengthening the shadows, which made it harder to see in the overgrown ground and tall trees. Except for the never-ending chattering of insects, silence surrounded them. Maybe they'd gotten away.

Something snapped behind them.

"We need to keep moving," Kellan whispered pulling her forward again.

She could hear whoever was chasing them. They weren't even trying to mask their footsteps. She had no idea who they were or what they wanted, but none of that mattered for the moment. Maneuvering across the uneven terrain with its thick flats and ridges was strenuous, and all that mattered was getting as far away from their pursuers as possible.

She scrambled across an overgrown slope, wishing they'd come to a trail. Instead, the ground suddenly gave way beneath her feet. She stifled a scream as her body slid down the steep incline, unable to stop as brush and small limbs slapped at her body. Her head hit something hard, bringing with it a stab of pain, but it was still another dozen or more yards before she hit the bottom of the ravine.

For a long moment, Tess didn't move. She had no idea how far she'd fallen. Heart pounding in her ears, she started moving slowly, terrified she might have broken something. Her legs worked, her arms worked, and the pain was minimal, but this was not the place where she wanted an emergency to happen. She worked to catch her breath, then rolled over, searching for Kellan in the shadows.

He was sitting a couple feet from her, moving timidly like she had. Trying to figure out if anything was broken.

"Kellan?"

He slid off his backpack then scooted toward her. "Are you okay?"

"I think so." She held up her hand. "A bit shaky."

"I'm so sorry."

Her chest heaved both from being winded and from the fear. "I don't know what's going on, but being shot at twice in one day does not leave a good feeling in my gut."

He glanced up the steep ravine that had taken them by surprise. "We need to keep moving."

She listened for the tell-tale sounds of whoever had chased them, not sure she could run again even if she had to. She might not have broken anything, but no doubt she was going to be sore in the morning.

He helped her to her feet, holding on to her a few additional seconds while she struggled to find her balance. Whatever she'd been drugged with seemed to have affected not only her memory, but her equilibrium as well.

Kellan handed her the beanie, reminding her how thankful she was—not for the first time—that she wasn't alone.

"You warm enough?" he asked. "Temperatures are

dropping, which is another reason we need to keep moving. I'm afraid a winter storm might be coming."

Great.

"I'll be fine." She put her beanie back on, then zipped up her jacket. "For now."

She forced herself to follow Kellan through the tall undergrowth for what seemed like hours to her still hazy mind. The brain fog had lifted—partially at least—but not enough for her to clearly see her muddled memories.

"I'm sorry," Tess said, leaning over, hands on her knees, struggling to catch her breath. "I'm still so tired."

"You're fine," Kellan said. "Catch your breath, then it looks like there might be a sheltered clearing not far ahead that will give us a view of the surrounding terrain. If they are following us, we need to be able to see them coming. And it will give you a chance to rest."

Tess took in a few slow breaths, trying desperately not to let fear's grip tighten further. So far, there had been no signs that whoever had shot at them was following. They were safe. For now, anyway.

A moment later, she followed Kellan to a small clearing that overlooked the dark clouds rolling across the valley below them. The spot was sheltered on three sides by tall trees and backed into the rock face that soared above them twenty-five or thirty feet.

"This is perfect," she said, sitting down on the ground and leaning back against the rock.

She gave into the fatigue and closed her eyes. If she could just rest for a little while, she'd be ready to keep going.

An unwanted memory surfaced.

Tess frowned. She might have forgotten some the

details of what had happened at Walter's house, but she did remember one thing that happened afterward.

She opened her eyes. "I need to apologize."

Kellan sat on a downed log across from her. "Apologize?"

She stared at the surrounding brush, avoiding his gaze. "I said some. . .inappropriate things when you first found me. I feel like the drug is wearing off, but I wasn't trying to come on to you. Or at least I wouldn't have if my head hadn't been messed with."

"You have nothing to apologize for. Shoot, you told me I was cute—or rather handsome." He shot her a wide grin. "I can't exactly complain about that."

"I'm sure there are other things I said that I can't even remember. It's just a bit—okay, a lot—embarrassing." She looked away again, needing to change the subject. "I'll be the first to say that I'm grateful you found me, but what are we supposed to do now?"

"We might have lost our horses, but I still have my backpack. Which means we have some food and water and a first-aid kit, which we're going to need for your knee."

She looked down at the hole in her jeans, matted with blood, and winced. "I hadn't even felt it."

He stepped in front of her, then slowly pulled away the ripped fabric, revealing a two-inch scrape from the fall. "I don't think it's as bad as it looks."

He grabbed his backpack, set it next to him and pulled out a small first-aid kit.

Tess knew that if he was anything like her, he needed a practical way to deal with the situation. Something he could fix.

"We always travel with water, hardtack and dried fruit,

coffee, and a couple of MREs for emergencies," he said, dousing the cut in disinfectant.

She squeezed her eyes shut for a moment, trying to ignore the sting. "Just in case you rescue a damsel in distress and then get shot at by an unknown assailant?"

He laughed. "I don't mind the rescuing the damsel in distress part."

She felt her face flush as she quickly shifted the conversation. "My family's going to be worried. My brothers and my father don't like it when I go out alone, but the reality is I can't be escorted everywhere. It's not practical."

He pulled out a small tube of cream and started dabbing it on the wound. "I guess they taught you to shoot?"

"When you come from a family of lawmen and ranchers, that pretty much comes with the territory. My dad had me target practicing when most kids were joining soccer and football teams."

"Somehow, I'm not at all surprised."

She watched as he screwed the lid back on the tube. "You do know the way back to Shadow Ridge, don't you?"

Kellan hesitated a moment too long.

"Kellan. . ."

"I can make an educated guess, thanks to the sun, but. . .honestly, I'm not sure where we are." He dropped the cream back into the kit, then picked up a bandage. "My worry is that it'll be dark before we get there. And that's without getting lost."

Tess's jaw tensed. That wasn't the answer she was hoping for. She looked around the small alcove while he finished bandaging her knee. So far there had been no sign again of the men after them, but while she understood his logic, they needed to get back to Shadow Ridge.

"So what do we do?" she finally asked.

"Camp out here for the night—"

"Wait." She pulled away from him, not prepared for his response. "I don't know if that's the wisest move. Not with the shooter—or shooters—still out there."

"I wish we had options, but I think we need to stay put and find our way to Shadow Ridge in the morning."

She had no reason not to trust Kellan, but that didn't mean she was comfortable with the idea. "There's got to be another option. There aren't a lot of people living out here, but if we can find somebody who knows the way—"

"And if we don't? What we don't need is to get lost out here when it's dark."

She let out a sharp breath, then nodded. She knew he was right, but whether it was the situation or simply the aftereffects of the drug, her anxiety was still raging.

She stood up and brushed off her pants. "What if they find us?"

"It's a possibility."

Tess frowned, not liking their odds. "What about a perimeter trip alarm?"

"Sounds like you are your father's daughter." He grabbed his backpack. "I should have something in here that we can use. The sheriff's always been a bit of a survivalist and makes sure we're prepared if we ever go out on our own. Matches, food, duct tape, and para cord. . ." He paused. "The para cord should be exactly what we need to set a perimeter alarm."

She shivered, as much from fear as from the dropping temperatures.

He frowned. "I'm sorry. I know this isn't what you want."

She forced a smile, not wanting him to know what she was really feeling. "It's fine."

Except it wasn't fine. Nothing was fine. The combination of knowing someone was someone after them, and that someone had drugged her, terrified her. And if she closed her eyes all she could see was Walter's dead body.

"You're not okay. You're shaking." Kellan pulled a wool blanket out of the bottom of his pack and shook it out. "I'll get a fire going along with some coffee first. You need to warm up."

"You don't have to baby me. My head's clearing. And with a fire they'll see the smoke."

He wrapped the striped blanket around her shoulders. "That's why I'm going for a smokeless fire."

It hadn't rained here for a while, which made it possible. Her father had taught her the basic idea that high levels of oxygen combined with certain dry fuels made an almost smokeless fire, but if those men found them. . .

"Hey. . .It's going to be okay." He rested his hand on her arm for a moment. "It looks as if they've lost our trail, and as soon as the sun comes up, we'll make our way back to Shadow Ridge. Trust me."

She nodded, but still couldn't shake the fear closing in around her. "I'm just. . .I'm worried that my father and my brothers are going to send out a search team. They'll see what happened at Walter's place and think the worst."

He motioned for her to sit back down. "Which is why I'm going to get you home as soon as I can. I promise."

The intensity in his gaze as he looked at her worked like a salve against the fear, even as he turned away to start gathering small twigs for the fire.

She watched as he lit the tinder, then slowly fed the flickering orange flames with the twigs he'd collected, Her father would be impressed with his skills. Kellan was level-headed, smart, and intuitive. Someone she'd enjoy getting to know more. Especially when he pulled out a portable percolator, fulfilling his promise of coffee. By the time he had the trip wire set up around their makeshift camp, the steamy drink was ready.

She took a sip from the mug he gave her and smiled, relishing the warmth of the drink. "Okay, I have to admit I'm not much of a coffee drinker, but this. . .this is the best coffee I've ever had."

He let out a low chuckle. "That's only because you're cold, tired, and hungry."

She matched his laugh, but something about him put her at ease. Something that made her believe everything really was going to turn out okay, and he'd figure out a way to get the two of them back home.

"Now that you've warmed up," he said, "are you hungry?"

"You really are prepared, aren't you?"

He smiled, then pulled out a couple of MREs. "Chili with beans, or Cheese tortellini. Your choice."

"I have to say, I'm impressed," she said, studying the shiny wrapping. "How about the pasta?"

"It's yours," he said, ripping open the first of the pouches. "They'll be hot in a few minutes."

"Can I ask you a question?" she asked after he finished

activating the meals and setting them against a rock to heat.

"Of course."

"Why were you going to Shadow Ridge?"

"I need to speak to your brothers."

"About?"

He hesitated before looking up and catching her gaze. "I found someone with information on why the grid went down. An FBI agent traveling to the capital."

"What?" Tess set her mug on the ground. News from outside the area had been sparse. No one knew why the grid had gone down, but if Kellan had answers. . .

"The problem is," he continued, "our source was injured badly and didn't make it. He left us with more questions than answers."

Tess leaned forward. "There's got to be a way to find out what he knew. Surely he wasn't traveling by himself."

"He wasn't. That's why I was headed to your brothers. The agent's team was ambushed, but there's still a chance to find the men he was traveling with. If they're still alive. They had a flash drive with sensitive information on it."

"Do you think it's possible to stop whoever's behind all of this?"

She rarely allowed herself to think about that question, because it only led to disappointment. The only way she'd learned to find peace in this new world was to accept its reality. Especially when there was nothing she could do about it.

"I definitely think it's possible, though I guess it depends on who's behind it and how much damage has been done." He took another sip of his coffee. "What's the first thing you would do if the power went back on?"

"I'd take a hot shower."

"Wow, no hesitation in that answer."

"Absolutely not. What about you?"

"Honestly, I'm not sure I can choose just one. A shower would be at the top of the list. I'd like to contact a few friends, and I could really go for a double cheeseburger with bacon."

"I don't know if I can talk about delicious food right now. I'm too hungry. I really miss my mother's macaroni and cheese, and my grandmother's pot roast with potatoes and carrots. And don't even get me thinking about pepperoni pizza, Dr Pepper, and ranch dressing."

"Root beer and Chinese takeaway."

She laughed as she ran her finger around the rim of the mug, finally starting to warm up. "It's interesting how my *needs* have shifted. The first few months, I had a list a mile long of things I was going to get as soon as the grid went back up. Somehow the weeks turned into months, and my priorities started to shift. I guess no matter how hard it is, we somehow just. . .adapt."

"So you don't crave pizza anymore?" he asked.

"I wouldn't go that far." Tess chuckled softly under her breath. "But it definitely has changed my perspective on what's important. Family. . .friends. . .faith."

She took another sip of the coffee, more anxious than ever to get home. She might not have expected his reason for going to Shadow Ridge, but that information only added to the question of who was after them. Was it someone connected with Walter's death? Or was it someone trying to stop Kellan from finding the information he was looking for?

CHAPTER EIGHT

KELLAN GLANCED across the small fire pit he'd made, waiting for the MREs to finish heating, and studied Tess as she sipped her coffee beneath the wool blanket. He really liked her. In fact, he'd liked her from the moment they'd first met a few weeks ago in Shadow Ridge. She was smart, compassionate, and beautiful. But he'd meant what he'd said to Miles. He might not have been able to put her out of his mind, but a relationship between the two of them wasn't possible. Even if she felt the way he did.

His biggest concern right now was that he'd made the wrong decision in staying here for the night, even though his concerns were valid. Maybe they could have made it back to Shadow Ridge before dark, but at least here they had a temporary shelter, and he didn't have to worry about getting lost in the dark.

Thanks to the sheriff, they had food and water, but he couldn't shake the worry over who was out there looking for them. He'd seen the fear in Tess's eyes, and he couldn't blame her. He knew hardly anything, but the facts that he did know were disturbing enough. Tess had been both shot at and drugged. He had a dead FBI agent and was searching for missing classified information. Although there didn't seem to be a connection between the two situations, it was enough to know that someone was after one or both of them.

He got up from the log where he'd been sitting and felt the heat in the warming packets. "Another four or five minutes and they'll be done."

"No problem. Can I ask you another question?"

He nodded, then went back to sit down on the log.

"Why law enforcement?"

He picked up his coffee mug, hesitating for a moment with his answer. "My father was in and out of prison most of my childhood. I pretty much wanted to be the opposite of who he was."

"Wow. I'm sorry."

He stared at his empty coffee cup. "Not the answer you expected, I guess."

"I'm not sure what I expected. Just. . .curious." She stretched her legs out in front of her, then pulled the blanket across her thighs. "Do you have contact with him at all? Before the Quake, I mean."

"It's been five. . .maybe six years since I saw him."

"I'm sorry if I'm being too personal."

"No. It's fine. Really. My father wasn't the only reason I went into law enforcement. When I was seventeen, there was a drive-by shooting. A friend was killed right in front of me. That bullet wasn't even meant for him. It impacted me, a reminder that life could and did change in an instant. I realized for the first time that I wasn't invincible."

"What about your mom?"

"She died when I was six. So I don't really remember her. Just fuzzy memories of her smile. I went to live with my grandmother for a while, then with my father for a couple of years until he went back to prison. I pretty much got tossed around to anyone would take me."

"That had to be hard."

He nodded. "I got in trouble a lot in high school, but a school counselor made me his project. Pulled me aside one day and told me I'd end up like my father if I didn't get my act together. But he also managed to convince me that that was not inevitable."

He was surprised how comfortable he was talking to her. The Quake had done more than just take the grid down and change their way of life. It had been an equalizer. A unifier in many ways. While there were still plenty of people who did their best to take advantage of the situation, it didn't matter what you'd had before the Quake. Everyone, on some level, was suffering. Everyone now had to figure out how to feed their children and how to keep warm at night, and for a lot of people that meant teaming up with neighbors and working together as a community. That was the part he was grateful for.

"So do you have any family out here?" she asked.

"Fork or spoon?" Kellan grabbed a couple utensils from his pack and held them up. "Fork or spoon."

"I suppose a fork for pasta."

Kellan handed it to her, then picked up her dinner pouch. "I lost my grandmother a few months ago. And as for my father. . .I have no idea where he is."

"There's not a single person who hasn't been touched by all of this, is there?" she said.

Silence hovered between them as he readied her pouch, the orange flames brighter as the sun sank beneath the horizon. He knew she understood. The loss. The loneliness. All the dreams put on hold.

"We've all lost someone," he said finally. "You lost your mother."

He watched the corners of her mouth tighten as he handed her the bag of pasta. "Careful. It's hot."

"We also don't know where my brother Sam is," she said. "He was supposed to come back to Shadow Ridge last Christmas for my parents' anniversary. He must've missed a flight, because he never made it." She stuck her fork inside the packet, but didn't take a bite. "Sometimes I feel like I've lost my mom *and* my dad."

"I've heard enough about your father to know that he lost a lot."

She looked up at him. "He talked to me last night about my mother. First time he's talked—I mean really talked—to me in months. He seems so lost. And guilty about not being there for me. I know he misses Mom. Worries about where Sam is. It's hard to know how to help him."

"You're carrying a lot."

"We all are." She stabbed a piece of pasta, finally taking a bite while he opened up his packet.

"How is it?"

She shot him a smile. "Good enough to make me very grateful I'm not out here alone."

"Thanks to the sheriff. He has quite a stash of military

and survival goods. And as for your dad. Give him time. He'll continue to heal. And be grateful, not only for the memories you have with him, but second chances to create even more as he heals."

"I know you're right. I used to love watching crime shows with my dad. Probably more to hear his reaction than actually watching the shows. He's always been so. . .old school." She smiled. "He thinks modern technology has its place—or at least used to—but there's nothing like good old-fashioned detective work."

"There is something to be said about human instinct. Did you ever think about going into law enforcement?"

She shook her head, then reached to take a sip of her coffee. "Never. I'm the free spirit in my family."

"Maybe, but I've seen your composite photos of crime scenes. You're really good."

She pulled the blanket tighter around herself and frowned. "Drawing crime scene photos isn't exactly how I want to spend my time."

"Do you still draw in your spare time?"

"I think I've forgotten what spare time is." She flicked an ant off her boot. "The only drawing I've actually done in the past few months is for my brothers. Somehow, sketching murder scenes zapped my creativity."

"Sorry to hear that because I'd really love to see some of your drawings." He took another bite of his chili, realizing that this time he was the one who'd hit too close to home. "You don't have to stop creating just because of the situation we're in. It might actually end up being therapeutic."

She poked her fork in her pasta, then set the meal

down. "When Jeremiah Daniels was murdered in our town, my brother called me in to make drawings of the crime scene. I had never been around death. Not beyond our animals on the ranch. Art had always been an escape for me. A way to express things inside me that I didn't know how to say."

"And now?"

"Every time I look at a piece of paper all I can see are the crime scenes I've sketched. My perspective of the world has changed forever. It was one thing to watch cop shows where the good guys always win, but this. . ." She leaned forward and rested her elbows on her thighs. "Death. Loss. Pain. I've seen so much of it."

"Why don't you just tell your brothers how you feel?"

"Because on one hand I wish I could run away and escape the reality of death and what one person can do to another, but on the other hand, helping them makes me feel as if I'm doing something to help make things right in this world."

"I understand, though I'd still love to see some of the things you've drawn."

"Maybe." She shrugged. "I don't show very many people my artwork."

He finished the last bite of his chili, then dropped the spoon inside the pouch and set it down. In trying to get to know her better, he'd pushed too hard in the wrong direction, not realizing how she'd react. She'd gone through enough today. The last thing he wanted was to dredge up unwanted memories.

"I heard a rumor that you make a mean pecan pie," he said.

The shift in the conversation brought a smile to her face. "I do, actually."

"That happens to be my favorite."

He put out the small fire as they continued talking, enjoying her smile once again, but worried now that darkness was falling that the orange flames would draw attention to their location. Slowly, the stars emerged from their hiding place, until the Milky Way, the Pleiades star cluster, and thousands of more stars hovered above them.

She yawned.

"You need to get some sleep, Tess. The drug's effects are probably still lingering."

She yawned again. "I'm fine."

"Then tell me more about the water system you've been working on."

Kellan glanced at her when she didn't answer. She'd fallen asleep against the rock, still bundled up in her coat and the wool blanket he'd given her. Her chest slowly rose and fell as the moon gave her face a silvery glow. He got up and pulled the blanket higher around her shoulders. He needed to check the perimeter, and make sure whoever had shot at them wasn't out there.

KELLAN SAT up and stretched his back as the first glow of sunrise began to break over the horizon. His muscles were sore and stiff after yesterday's fall down the ridge, making it painful to move. But they couldn't sit and wait around today. With the first rays of light filtering above the horizon, they needed to get moving and find their way back to Shadow Ridge.

Tess still lay sound asleep a couple of feet from where he sat. He almost hated to wake her up. She looked so peaceful. Waking her up would bring with it the reminder of everything that had happened. Thankfully, he'd seen no sign of any intruders—animal or human. He should be able to figure out the direction they needed to go from the sun, though he still wasn't sure exactly where they were. The run through the forest and drop over the ridge had left him disoriented. As long as they didn't run into the bad guys first, hopefully he could get them both back to Shadow Ridge in the next few hours. He watched as she rolled over and opened her eyes.

"Hey, sleepyhead."

She let out a soft groan. "What time is it?"

"About time to get moving."

She pushed the blanket off and sat up. "Wow, I'm sore."

"Me too. That fall did quite a number on both of us."

"You didn't stay up all night, did you?"

"I dozed some."

"Good, but I'm sorry. And I had your blanket."

"It's okay." He pointed to the shiny emergency blanket from his pack. "I stayed warm enough, and nobody found us last night. I'm hoping we can get you back to Shadow Ridge by lunch. Except. . ."

"What's wrong?"

"That heavy cloud bank is intensifying, and with the wind picking up, I think we're definitely looking at another winter storm."

It was just another one of the millions of things that frustrated him about the grid going down. There was no way to listen to a weather report on radio or TV to know what was coming. And while he was no expert on reading the weather, if he was right, they might end up going from one dangerous situation straight into another.

CHAPTER NINE

TESS MANAGED to stand up then started folding up the blanket Kellan had given her. Although her head had almost cleared, her body ached from the fall down the ridge. She was surprised she'd been able to sleep at all. Her father and brothers all loved camping. She was the one who'd always managed to get out of the overnight trips. It wasn't as if she didn't appreciate the beauty of the surrounding desert and mountains, but she'd take a good night's sleep in her own bed any day over a sleeping bag and a tent. Last night, she hadn't had either.

"How did you sleep?" he asked, taking the folded blanket from her.

"That's questionable." She stifled a yawn. "The only reason I know I slept was because of the weird dreams. I was back in elementary school, and the teacher kept making me say the alphabet over and over."

"That's a bit odd." He flashed her that smile that always managed to make her heart drop a beat. "Maybe the drug hasn't completely worn off."

"I wouldn't doubt it." She glanced past him to the fire pit he'd made the night before. "You don't happen to have any more coffee in that pack of yours, do you?"

"I found a couple of MRE instant packs, and they're already heating. It's not Starbucks, but—"

"It'll be perfect." This time she matched his smile. "I'm going to need something to get me going this morning."

She rubbed the back of her neck, trying to erase some of the tension that had built up overnight. The dream had been strange. She would have expected someone to have been chasing her. Instead, it was as if her mind had been trying to solve a puzzle.

Letters.

Tess reached into her coat pocket for Walter's notebook, grateful she still had it. Her mind finally made the connection. There had been cryptic letters in Walter's notebook.

"Tess. . .are you okay?"

"Yeah, I was just thinking about my dream and the letters. This is Walter's notebook," she said, holding it up. "I'm not even sure why I grabbed it when I was at his house, but it seemed. . . I don't know. Personal. Something I didn't want just anyone to go through."

"The two of you were friends?"

"We were," she said, not missing the sympathetic tone in his question. "He was lonely. His wife passed away a few years ago and his daughters live out of state. I pass his house every time I go into town, so I got in the habit of checking in on him a couple of times a week. He seemed to enjoy the company."

"I'm not surprised. I think loneliness is one of the saddest consequences of the Quake."

Tess flipped through the pages, stopping at the odd notes she'd seen at Walter's house. Kellan was right. The grid going down left a large percentage of the population stranded. It was a difficult situation. Churches and communities, along with law enforcement, tried their best to help those in need, but there were still many who fell through the cracks.

And even though she'd tried to visit Walter as much as she could, she couldn't keep from feeling guilty that he'd died alone.

"He was always writing things down," she said, pulling her thoughts back to the present. "To-do lists, reminders, even the weather and his visitors." She flipped through the pages until she found what she was looking for. "But I found this. There are three pairs of letters, and the word *cover-up* is circled. There's also an X that's underlined."

"We've still got a couple minutes until the coffee is ready. I can try to help." Kellan took the notebook from her and glanced over the page. "The first thing that comes to mind is that a pair of letters could be someone's initials."

"I thought the same thing," she said, following him to the downed log and sitting next to him. "Years ago, Walter was a private investigator in Dallas. And if you look through the notebook, he has his own shorthand language. It wouldn't surprise me at all if he was investigating something."

"That makes sense," Kellan said, looking at Walter's notes.

She stood up, feeling restless, and started pacing.

Kellan tapped on the book with his finger. "You mentioned arsenic has been found in your water source."

"That's what my sister believes. Yes."

"What if the AS isn't a who, but a what. The symbol for arsenic is AS."

Tess stopped pacing and sat back down next to him. "Chemistry wasn't my favorite subject, but I should have thought of that. Maybe he was questioning the recent arsenic deaths."

"It's hard to read his handwriting." He turned the notebook sideways, then back again. "What if this isn't an X? To me it looks more like a sideways X, or crossbones."

"A symbol of death?" A shiver slid down her spine as she took the book back from him. "What if he found out something and was killed for it?"

"As a sheriff's deputy, I'm not sure you have enough evidence to make that conclusion, but on the other hand, his house was shot at and you were drugged."

"Jared Palmer." The name came to mind as the pieces started coming together. "JP."

"Who's that?"

"He and his wife, Raelynn, both recently died from what Hope believes to be arsenic poisoning from the water."

"So now we have JP and RP. But if there was some kind of cover-up, why wouldn't Walter just go to the police?"

"I don't know, but maybe he was trying to get more information. Something more solid before he went to the authorities."

"What about Walter himself?" Kellan asked. He opened the pouches and poured the coffee into the mugs they'd used the night before. "You said you thought he died from arsenic poisoning?"

"From what I saw, there were definite signs of poisoning. The strange thing is that Walter was using a filter for his water. Filters we believed were working. Plus, I saw him a few days ago and he was fine. Which makes me worry now that the filter isn't working like we'd hoped."

"What about the couple who died?" Kellan asked, handing her one of the mugs. "Did they have a filter for their water?"

"No. Which was another reason why we thought the filter was working. No one who had a filter showed signs of being sick. Not until Walter."

"I don't know." Kellan sat down next to her, then took a sip of his drink. "Knowing what we do, it doesn't seem that much of a stretch to believe that Walter stumbled onto something he shouldn't have."

"You mean murder."

Tess took a sip of the hot drink, but barely tasted it. She didn't want the theory to be right. Walter started poking around and discovered that somebody was trying to cover up a murder by blaming arsenic poisoning from the water. He likely asked one too many questions. . .and became a target for murder himself.

She glanced around her. The wind rippled through the trees. Birds called out and answered each other. There was a partial view of the valley from where they'd stayed protected for the night, but she didn't feel safe. She felt vulnerable and lost, and if it hadn't been for Kellan finding her, she might not even be alive.

She tried to shove away the fear that had rooted itself in her gut. Maybe she was crazy to even consider the scenario that Walter had been murdered, but she hadn't imagined the things that had happened to her. Something had happened at Walter's house.

Kellan cradled the mug in his hands, the concern back in his eyes. "You okay?"

"It's debatable. I'm ready to get home."

"I agree. Because there are definitely a lot of questions, and until we get back to Shadow Ridge, I'm not sure we're going to find the answers we need."

"Unless someone is still after me."

"Let's not start borrowing trouble," Kellan said. "Knowing that someone is after us is enough. We'll sort out the whys later. But until then, we need to finish this coffee, pack up, and get moving."

She knew he was right. Worrying about what might happen wasn't productive. They just needed to get back to Shadow Ridge and then, together with her brothers, Hope, and her father, they'd figure out the truth.

A loud rustling in the trees to her left stopped her train of thought. Something—or someone—was out there.

"Kellan. . ."

"Stay where you are." He handed her his coffee, then pulled his sidearm out of its holster. "I'll be right back."

She looked around as he disappeared into the thick brush surrounding them, then picked up a thick, club-like limb lying on the edge of the clearing. For a short time during their conversation, she'd almost been able to forget what had happened and why they were here. Now the adrenaline was surging and the vulnerability had returned. The back of her head pounded, brought on, she was sure, from a night sleeping on the ground and the fading effects of whatever had drugged her.

She turned around at another rustling noise and held her makeshift weapon higher. For the first time, she wished she had not only listened to her father's survival skill speeches, but that she'd advanced further in the defense training classes she'd taken. She'd never been interested in anything more than short hikes in the mountains, where she could snap some photos and sketch them later. She glanced back where Kellan had disappeared into the trees. He clearly had survival skills, but what if they weren't enough? She stepped closer to the tree line, searching for the source of the noise. As her anxiety soared, she started praying.

God, I hate that every time I come to You I'm always in a crisis. All I know is that this feels like a major crisis. I'm scared. Feeling alone. And really need a way out of this.

Something hooted, and then she saw it. An owl swooped down at her, managing a sharp tug on her ponytail. Tess swung the club as she ducked. She pressed her lips together. She couldn't scream. She didn't want to make her location known if *they* were out there, but another hoot, and then a flash of white whooshed as the owl dive-bombed her again.

"Tess. . .what are you doing?"

Club still held high above her head, she spun around as the owl disappeared into the trees. "Kellan?"

"It's okay. There's no one out there." She didn't miss the hint of amusement on his face. "Just an owl that I see you've already discovered."

She dropped the club to her side, feeling foolish. "It's really not funny."

"Not at all." He held his hand up, still fighting not to laugh. "I'm sorry. I shouldn't laugh, but seeing you swinging that stick to ward off an owl. . ."

She touched her messed-up ponytail, grateful that her

hair was all those sharp talons had managed to grab, but still embarrassed.

"It's not uncommon for owls to attack humans," Kellan said, reholstering his gun. "From what I've heard, they especially like buns and ponytails."

"You might as well laugh," she said, starting to feel an unexpected surge of relief. "I guess it's better to battle it out with a flying fowl than an armed gunman."

"True, though I am sorry." He didn't even try to hold back his amusement this time. "I needed a good laugh this morning."

She couldn't help but smile back. "Glad to help."

He dropped his hands to his side, his smile still broad, and caught her gaze. "Seriously, though, are you okay?"

She nodded, then quickly retied her ponytail before picking up her beanie.

"Best I can figure, we're southwest of Shadow Ridge, and when I was out scouting just now, I found a trail heading in that direction."

"That's good news."

"Very good news." He stepped toward her, then reached down and squeezed her hands. "I'm going to get you home safe. I promise."

She looked at him, suddenly aware of the intensity in his gaze. No matter how hard she tried, she couldn't shake the effect he had on her. If she was honest with herself, she wasn't sure she wanted to.

THE SUN HAD FULLY RISEN by the time they'd packed up their makeshift camp and found the trail Kellan had discovered, but one of the growing concerns was the falling temperature. The stunning cliff-top views of flatter terrain ahead framed by distant mountains helped lift some of the layers of fear as they hiked the narrow footpath. But she wasn't ready to let her guard down. Not yet. Whoever had shot at her and drugged her was still out there. She wasn't going to feel safe again until she was back in Shadow Ridge.

But finding their way out of the valley wasn't as straightforward as she'd hoped. While her head seemed to have finally cleared, and she'd warmed up from matching Kellan's brisk pace, an emotional fatigue had settled in. The sun had almost reached its zenith, and still nothing looked familiar.

A cabin with a shaded veranda emerged ahead as they rounded a bend, nestled at the edge of an open spot of land. The place looked lived in and well kept, an off-the-grid home with solar panels, water storage, and several outdoor buildings including two shipping containers.

Tess let out a sigh of relief and followed Kellan up the path that led to the front door. "Now we just have to pray someone's home."

Kellan stopped in front of the door, knocked, then took a step back.

Seconds passed.

He knocked again. This time, an armed man with a scraggly beard, wearing an oversized flannel shirt and jeans, opened the door.

"Sorry to disturb you," Kellan started. "We ran into a bit of trouble out here—"

The man shifted his weapon, pointing it at them and stopping any further explanation. "The only kind of people I see out here are people who want trouble. So if you know what's good for you, you'll get off my land before I pull this trigger."

CHAPTER TEN

"HOLD ON." Kellan took a step back and held up his hands. "I'm a deputy with the Van Horn Sheriff's Department. We're not here looking for trouble. Just some help."

The man let the scope of his weapon drop a degree. "You're a deputy?"

Kellan pulled his badge out of his pocket, taking the question as a chance to explain their position. "Long story short, we were on our way to Shadow Ridge and ran into some trouble. We're looking for directions and maybe some hot coffee."

The man studied them for a moment as if he were trying to decide what he was going to do. But Kellan couldn't afford for the man to turn them away. With the temperature dropping, he was cold and knew Tess was as well.

"Like I said," Kellan pressed, "we're just lost and need to know which direction is Shadow Ridge."

"Sorry about the reaction. This rifle's the only thing between me and getting killed." He dropped the gun to his side. "Not sure you're going to make it to Shadow Ridge today. There's a storm coming. Winds are picking up, and there isn't a lot of shelter out here."

"We're sorry to be any trouble," Tess offered, but he didn't miss the disappointment in her voice.

"Don't worry about it. I could use some catching up on any news. It's been a long time since I've had company."

"We appreciate your hospitality, then." Kellan felt a wave of relief wash through him as he followed Tess inside.

"I don't have much, but I do have some coffee on the stove."

"That would be wonderful," Tess said, moving straight to the wood stove in the corner of the one-room cabin.

Inside, the setup was both simple and rustic. The left wall had been made into a small kitchen area with a couple of cupboards, a sink, wood stove, and minimal counter space. On the opposite wall was a twin bed covered in an old quilt. In between, was a worn recliner, a desk, and dozens of books tucked into bookshelves that went almost to the ceiling.

"I've got everything I need right here," the man said, placing his shotgun back above the door. "And it's Rick Evermore, by the way."

"Deputy Kellan Gray and this is Tess McQuaid."

"Nice to meet you both." Rick opened the door and pulled in another chair from the porch. "Like I said, I don't get a lot of company out here. Go ahead and sit down and I'll get you that coffee."

Rick started rummaging through the cupboard while Kellan took the chair he'd brought in and Tess moved the wooden desk chair closer to the stove. A minute later, Rick finished pouring the coffee that was simmering in a kettle, then handed a mug to Tess and one to Kellan.

"Thank you so much," she said, wrapping her fingers around the mug. "I might be able to finally warm up again."

Kellan took a couple of sips and let the hot drink flow through him. While he appreciated the coffee, situations like this—when he felt totally out of control—frustrated him. There was no way to communicate where he was. No way to let Tess's family know she was all right.

"Why are you out here in the first place?" Rick asked. "I'm assuming it has to be something serious for you to be traveling with a storm heading in."

Kellan took another sip, needing to be vague with his reply. "I was escorting Tess back to Shadow Ridge, and someone started shooting at us. We managed to evade them, but lost our horses in the process. With no GPS, I'm honestly not sure how far out we are."

"It's a different world we live in, even for me," Rick said, pouring himself a cup before settling into the recliner. "I like living this way, but I used to have my online groups I'd chat with. Don't have any of that anymore."

"Looks like you've got a pretty good setup here." Tess unzipped her coat and scooted a few inches away from the wood stove. "Already living off the grid gives you a huge advantage."

Rick shrugged and looked around. "I get by. Knew this would happen one day. But enough about me. Get yourself warmed up with some coffee, and then you can decide what you want to do. You're still a good three hours on foot from Shadow Ridge, and that's without running into the storm."

"Thank you," Tess said. "We appreciate it."

Kellan glanced at Tess. He agreed, but his frustration was mounting. It wasn't wise to try to get to Shadow Ridge right now, but the last thing he wanted to do was spend another night out here. He needed to get Tess home to her family.

"What's the latest news?" The older man leaned forward. "It's been a while since I talked to anybody. Believe it or not, it was several weeks before I knew about the blackout. Just thought my internet had gone out until I went into town for supplies. Then I thought I'd missed the end of the world."

"That's a pretty good description," Tess said.

"You're law enforcement. You've had to have seen the worst of it."

"A lot of thefts, as you would imagine," Kellan said. "We've taken down several gangs who were stealing and selling on the black market. Human trafficking's on the rise, but there's also a renewed sense of community."

"That's something that's been missing for a long time." Rick leaned forward, seemingly ready to soak up anything they could tell him. "Any word on what's happening across the country?"

"Unfortunately, we have far more questions than answers."

Rick shook his head. "You have to know something after all this time."

"I wish we did," Kellan said. "We know it's widespread, but beyond what's happening in this county, your guess is as good as mine."

"In Shadow Ridge, we're starting to see some commerce take place," Tess said. "People are selling food and exchanging goods like eggs and seasonal vegetables."

Kellan glanced up at the window as Tess continued speaking. The storm clouds were moving in faster than he'd anticipated. They couldn't be that far from familiar territory, but was it worth the risk to push through and get Tess home today? Or was it better that they hunker down and wait out the storm, hoping it didn't last?

"Kellan. . .are you okay?"

He turned back to the conversation at Tess's question. "Yeah. Sorry. I was just watching the clouds. They're moving quickly."

Rick set his mug on the small table next to him. "Do you have any idea who's behind all this?"

"Unfortunately, no." Which was true. But he wasn't going to share about what had happened back in Van Horn. He hadn't even told Tess everything. "What about you? Any suspicious activity out here lately? Anyone coming around and stirring up trouble?"

"I've had a few run-ins with people, though not recently," Rick said. "Thankfully, I've always been able to protect myself, though I do wish I had a dog out here. Mine passed away recently, but I've found that a shotgun speaks for itself."

Tess frowned. "I'm sorry about your dog."

Rick nodded. "Me to."

"I guess all we can do is 'hope that real love and truth are stronger in the end than any the evil and misfortune in the world,'" Kellan said.

"Isn't that Dickens?" Tess asked.

"Yeah." Kellan's gaze shifted to the rows of books

across the room that looked primarily to be old classics with a number of Charles Dickens's works plus a few thick contemporary novels thrown in. "I noticed your collection. I had an English teacher who made us memorize literature quotes. For some reason that one stuck."

"An applicable quote for the world today," Rick said, heading to the sink to rinse out his mug. "Do you have any idea who shot at you?"

"No. Far as I know they didn't follow us, just set us way off course."

Rick wiped his hands on a towel, then turned back around. "Well, if you decide you don't want to face the weather, you're welcome to stay here for the night. It'll be cozy, but hopefully things will clear up tomorrow."

Kellan saw Tess's expression fall, and wished there was another solution. "I think he's right."

"I know. I just wish I could contact my family. And I don't want us to be an imposition."

"I could put you to work to earn your stay, if that would make you feel better." Rick chuckled. "I'm not sure how low the temperatures are going to drop. I've got the animals secured for the night, but I need to make sure there's enough wood to keep the fire going."

"Not a problem," Kellan said. "Though we might want to get started. Looks like there are already flakes falling."

"I see you've got some sourdough starter in the kitchen," Tess said.

"How's your biscuit-making skills?"

"Not bad. I can make some for dinner, if you'd like."

Rick's smile broadened. "It's been a long time since I've had someone cook for me, and I certainly wouldn't turn it down. Get tired of my boring fare. I have a can of sausage gravy in the cupboard. Everything you need should be there."

The wind had picked up and large flakes were falling by the time Kellan and Rick stepped outside. While he wished they were already back in Shadow Ridge, Kellan was grateful they'd found this place. Wandering around with inclement weather heading in would have been a risky situation. At least this way he'd be able to keep Tess safe another night.

"This is quite a setup," Kellan said, pulling on the gloves Rick had given him. "I'd love to hear more about your system. Looks like you know what you're doing. We've got some good sources, but we can always use more. Not all of us were as prepared as you."

"It's pretty simple, really." Rick rubbed his beard. "The greenhouse has worked great for growing produce. There's a barn for supplies, food storage, and my horses. Insulated glass to heat the water tank. Solar panels to run the swamp cooler and keep the fan circulating. There's a solar oven, several large water tanks set up for rainwater catchment, and a composting toilet."

"And all of this isn't too isolated for you?" Kellan asked.

"Chose this place because I can't see a neighbor from here. Mountains in the distance, but for the most part wide-open space filled with brush. Which is just the way I like it." Rick pulled a wood-splitter maul from a small storage bin and held it out. "Want to take the first swing?"

"Sure." Kellan set a log on a stump and swung the axe. Two more swings and the log split in two. It had been a long time since he'd chopped wood, but it didn't take long to get into a rhythm. He chopped while Rick supplied him with more logs and filled the wheelbarrow with the split ones.

"I envy you a bit," Kellan said as he reached for another log.

"Why's that?"

"The peace and quiet out here can't be bought." Kellan raised the axe, then swung down hard. "My job's been 24/7 since the moment the grid went down. Sometimes I feel like it's a never-ending battle."

"You almost make me feel guilty for leaving everything behind." Rick picked up another armful of chopped wood and laughed. "Almost."

Kellan pulled a bandana out of his pocket and wiped the sweat off his brow and the back of his neck. He glanced at the surrounding landscape, wondering what it would be like to walk away from his job and focus on having a family.

But he was getting sidetracked on a pipe dream.

There was a mound of dirt about twenty feet to his left, recently dug, and the size of a grave.

"That's where I buried my dog," Rick said, grabbing another pile of wood. "He was with me for ten years."

"I'm sorry."

"Me too. But he's not the only thing I've lost this past year. I've learned from experience that there's no escaping death in this new world."

Kellan looked back at the grave, wondering what the man's story was, and felt the threads of vulnerability tighten at his statement. Truth was, there hadn't been a way to escape death in the old world either.

CHAPTER ELEVEN

TESS STIRRED from where she was lying and opened her eyes. The orange glow from the flickering flames of the wood stove caught her attention. She fought for a moment to remember where she was, but it didn't take long this time for the memories of the last two days to flood her mind. Kellan finding her, getting shot at, spending the night out under the stars, and then finding this cabin. Wind whipped against the roof of the small house, making her grateful for the bed she was sleeping on, but also reminding her that she was still no closer to home than she'd been yesterday. And no closer to letting her family know she was safe.

After chopping wood, Kellan and Rick had returned with enough fuel to get them through the cold night, and she'd managed to serve up some decent biscuits and gravy. The two men had spent a couple hours playing chess while she'd browsed the small library and started reading a book Rick told her she could keep. He'd also peppered Kellan with more questions of what was going on *out there* as they battled it out on the board.

Now, Rick snored quietly in the recliner while Kellan sat next to the mat he'd been sleeping on. She rolled to her side, raised her head, and rested her chin on her hand. The soft glow of the fire highlighted his silhouette, reminding her of something else.

She was falling for the handsome deputy.

Or maybe she was already there.

He must have sensed her staring at him because a moment later, he looked up and smiled at her. He crossed the room, then sat down on the edge of the bed.

"I'm sorry," he whispered. "I didn't mean to wake you up."

"It wasn't you. My mind won't stop racing."

"You're not the only one whose mind is racing. You doing okay?"

From the other side of the room, Rick shifted in the chair, then a moment later started snoring again.

"Like you," he said, "I have a few things on my mind. But you need to try and go back to sleep. We'll need all our strength to make it back to Shadow Ridge."

She tightened her grip on her blanket. "And if the weather doesn't improve?"

"Then we'll deal with that. I need to get you home. Your family must be worried about you. I'm sure half the town is out looking for you."

She sat up, leaned against the wall, and tugged the blanket around herself. "Which is one of the reasons I can't sleep."

"And the other reason?"

"I'm cold."

He grabbed the blanket he'd been using and scooted up next to her against the wall before wrapping his arm around her shoulders and pulling her against him.

He was warm, but more than that, he stirred something inside her.

Something that wasn't going to work.

"Better?" he asked.

"Yes."

Much.

Until he got her home, then headed back to Van Horn. That was why this—whatever she was feeling—wasn't going to work.

"Do you ever feel like you're just holding your breath. . .waiting for things to go back to normal?" he asked.

She caught his gaze, trying not to notice the intensity of his blue eyes, or the strength of his hands. "What do you mean?"

"Sometimes I feel like I'm just doing what I need to do to get by, but not really living. How do we make all of this our new normal that gives us a future? Family. . .kids. . .I'd still like to have all of that one day."

She looked away, not sure what he was implying. He was different from most of the guys she'd gone to school with. She'd noticed Gideon holding her gaze a little too long from time to time and had wondered if he was interested in her, but she knew she wasn't interested in him. Kellan, though, did something to her heart she'd never felt before. Something about him that managed to touch the recesses of her soul and make her want to open up.

"I have to believe that all this will be over at some point." She searched for the right words to convey what she was feeling. "But I also can't help but feel that maybe everything that's happened has changed us in a way for the better. The working together as a family and a community. That's something I don't want to go away."

She could feel the warmth of his arm around her and his heart beating in his chest against her.

"I need to bring in some more firewood from the porch," he said. "The fire's going down."

She pressed her hand against his arm. "Can I ask you a question first?"

"Sure."

"There's been a change in you, ever since you came back in from chopping wood. You've been. . .distant. Worried about something, and it's more than me or the weather, isn't it?"

She tried to read his expression in the shadowy light of the fire, hoping she hadn't overstepped her place. It was strange how the past twenty-four hours had made her feel as if she'd known him her entire life.

And something was wrong.

Kellan glanced at Rick, who was still snoring in his chair. "There are some things that aren't adding up here."

"What do you mean?"

"I just can't help but wonder if he's really who he says he is," he whispered, catching her gaze in the firelight.

She looked past him, confused. "What do you mean?"

"I'll admit, he's a little rough around the edges, but I don't think he's been living off the grid like he claims."

"I'm not sure I'm following you. Who do you think he is?"

"That's what I don't know. Yet."

She caught the fatigue in his eyes and wondered how much he'd actually slept in the past two nights. Add to that the emotional and physical strain he was under, and no wonder he was paranoid. Because there couldn't be any truth to his suspicions.

Or could there?

"I've spent time around people like him," Tess said. "He seems a lot like Walter. Someone who's used to being alone, and who's a bit. . .quirky. It doesn't mean they've got some hidden agenda going on."

"Maybe not, but take for instance, the book on the table by Dickens and half a dozen more on the shelves. He acted as if he'd never heard that quote I said."

Tess pulled away slightly. "So you don't trust the man because he didn't know a Dickens quote."

"No. . . Yes."

"Walter had a stunning glass chess set in his living room, and yet he'd never played chess. The only reason he had it was because it was his father's. He preferred word games."

"That's not the only thing he didn't know," Kellan rushed on. "He didn't recognize your name."

"Why should he?"

"The McQuaid name is legendary across the entire county. Everyone knows your father. In fact, I bet before the Quake, most people in Shadow Ridge and the outlying areas had his number on speed dial in case they needed help."

"That's true, but that doesn't really prove there's something suspect going on. This is a man who's lived off the grid for years and who's content with isolation."

"Why wait until a storm is hitting to fill up your woodpile?"

"He ran out," she said.

"Okay. How about this?" Kellan lowered his voice. "There's a grave out there, fifty feet from the house, behind the woodpile."

"His dog just died."

"And if it didn't? If that was just another lie?"

She crossed her arms. "Okay, let's go with your theory. If he's not the real homeowner, then who is he?"

Kellan hesitated. "I don't know."

"And if your theory's correct, then where's the real owner, and why would an imposter welcome us into his house, *especially* knowing you're a deputy?"

"Maybe to find out what I know."

She paused for a moment. While the scenario seemed unlikely, she had to admit it was possible.

"You think he's one of the men that shot your informant."

"Maybe. I'm not the only person looking for that flash drive, and we already know it's worth killing for."

A chill shuddered through her despite the warmth of his body heat next to her. She didn't want to believe there was any validity to his theory because that would change everything. No longer would they be safely sheltered in the middle of the desert. Her life—their lives—would be in the hands of a possible killer.

She glanced across the room to where Rick was still snoring softly in the recliner. "I don't know. I think it's more likely that he's just a lonely man who thankfully welcomed us into his house during a storm. There's nothing sinister about that."

"You're probably right," Kellan whispered back. "It wouldn't be the first time I let my Spidey sense get out of control, to where I was seeing things that weren't there."

She pressed her hand against his arm. "You did rescue me, which does make you a hero in my book."

"At least I got that right."

As far as she was concerned, he'd gotten everything right. He'd found her out there and kept her safe until now. She knew he'd do everything in his power to get her home safely.

"I really do need to go get some more wood from the porch," he said, breaking into her thoughts. "We can't let the fire die down."

She nodded, but neither of them moved. Her gaze dropped to his lips, and as inappropriate as it seemed, she suddenly wished very badly that he would kiss her. Except, falling for Kellan Gray felt as dangerous at the moment as his theory that they were being harbored by a fugitive. Because, in the end, she knew she was going to get her heart broken. That this—whatever she was feeling— wouldn't make it with the miles between them.

And the last thing she wanted was a broken heart.

"I'll leave you the blanket," he said, still not moving.

She nodded. "Bundle up before you go out."

He held her gaze for a few seconds more, then headed toward the door. Tess pulled the blanket up around her shoulders and turned toward the wall, not sure she was going to be able to sleep the rest of the night. Because not only was there the real possibility that the man on the other side of the room wasn't who he said he was, she knew she'd fallen head over heels for Kellan Gray. And she wasn't sure which one terrified her the most.

CHAPTER TWELVE

Tess was right. He was just being paranoid. Kellan grabbed his coat and weapon, then slipped outside and closed the door of the cabin as quietly as he could, not wanting to wake Rick. At least he wanted her to be right. He wasn't used to letting his emotions shove him into a corner, but maybe that was why he wasn't looking at the situation rationally. He felt the heavy responsibility of getting her home to her family and was fearful of missing something that might put her life at further risk. But was that paranoia triggering the doubts?

He glanced around the property he'd familiarized himself with earlier while chopping wood. Tess had given him answers to everything he'd thrown at her. For the Dickens' quote, the McQuaid name, and even the freshly dug grave. Maybe Rick Evermore was simply a man who'd chosen to live off-grid and do life on his own terms. There was nothing sinister about that. If Kellan were honest with himself, Tess McQuaid was the real linchpin that had set him off course the moment he encountered her again. No matter how hard he tried, he couldn't ignore his growing interest, how his heart beat faster when she was next to him, or how badly he'd wanted to kiss her a few minutes ago.

He tried to push away the tangled feelings gripping his heart as he shoved his hands into his pockets. He had no desire to have a long-distance relationship, and with his responsibilities back in Van Horn, and her family in Shadow Ridge, they didn't exactly have options. Not in a world without FaceTime calls and weekend visits. Right now, he needed to focus on whether or not he was on target with his doubts about Rick Evermore. Which meant bringing in more wood was going to have to wait.

Snow fell as he pulled a flashlight from his coat pocket and headed toward the barn. He couldn't be out here long, but he wanted to make a quick sweep of the property. He'd never had a problem keeping his emotions separate from his job, and it was time he got focused. Because that's all this was. A job. He'd found someone in distress, and he found a solution. It was time to stop allowing his emotions to get wrapped up with his responsibilities as a deputy, and that meant listening to his gut.

At least that was what he was trying to convince his heart of.

Kellan squeezed his grip on the flashlight, unsure of what he was looking for. Rick—if he was who he said he was—seemed to be knowledgeable of the property when they'd been out chopping wood. So what was it that kept nagging at him?

He glanced back at the house, praying the man didn't

wake up, then slipped inside the barn. Equipment sat to the right, and at the far end were two large tanks, filled with, he assumed, feed for the animals. There were two stalls for the horses where one was lying down. The other horse came up to him, looking for a treat.

"Hey. . ." Kellan let the horse nuzzle his shoulder while he swept his flashlight beam around the barn. "How are you doing, buddy?"

Although the stall needed cleaning, nothing looked out of place. He went back outside, then quickly checked the other outbuildings. The last place was the greenhouse that held a decent winter garden.

He was latching the door when a noise from inside the greenhouse caught his attention. He opened the door again and shifted the flashlight until he caught movement. A mouse scurried down one of the rows and out of sight.

Kellan let out a soft chuckle. There was no boogie man in here. No sign of foul play. Maybe it was time to drop his theory.

He started to close the door again when his flashlight caught something on the doorframe he hadn't seen before. A partial handprint of what looked like smeared blood. He crouched down next to it. There was no way to test the substance, but he'd bet anything that was what it was. But still. . .there were dozens of ways to get injured out here, and not all of them were life threatening or malicious.

There was only one way he was going to be able to dismiss his misgivings, and that was by finding out what was inside the grave.

The cabin still looked quiet as Kellan retrieved a shovel from the barn then headed for the newly dug gravesite. If he was wrong, he was going to have some explaining to do to their host, but if he was right. . .

Kellan stood over the freshly turned dirt, gripped the shovel, and started digging. A coyote howled in the distance, sending shivers down his spine and making him wonder how he'd suddenly become a grave robber. This was not the way he'd intended to spend his Friday night. He wished he was back in the cabin with Tess, getting to know her better. Wished that none of his suspicions had led him here.

It didn't take long for him to find something. A yellow piece of fabric emerged. Dropping to the ground, he started shoving the dirt aside with his fingers. Seconds later he unearthed a piece of clothing that looked to be part of a man's shirt. He tugged on the piece of cloth until it—and the arm it was attached to—broke free from the dirt. Kellan jumped back at the discovery, biting his tongue in the process. Blood pooled in his mouth as he moved more dirt aside. Another minute, and vacant eyes stared back at him. Kellan rolled up the sleeve and discovered an American flag tattoo. When he bared the corpse's chest, he saw the bullet hole.

Lawrence Haley.

But that wasn't all he found. Cigarette burns tracked across the man's torso.

Tess. He needed to get back to Tess.

When he pushed himself up, more of the dirt caved in, exposing an air pocket below the body. Kellan stumbled back from the edge then froze. A second body was wedged beneath the first. He quickly scooped away the dirt. The man's bearded face was rough and weathered by the sun. It was the face of someone who'd spent years of hard work in the middle of the desert. And it was confirmation that the man inside the cabin with Tess was an imposter.

Pulling his gun from his holster, Kellan took off for the house. Two bodies. One unquestionably murdered. He'd been foolish to leave her alone with that man. A man who, as far as he was concerned, was behind the death of both bodies in that grave.

Kellan tore around the corner of the barn, then froze. Rick—or whoever he really was—stepped off the porch, holding Tess with a gun to her head.

"You just couldn't leave it alone, could you?" the man said.

Moonlight caught the fear in Tess's eyes. "Kellan. . ."

Kellan held up his hands. "Unfortunately, I was right. This isn't Rick Evermore."

"Then who is he?" Tess's voice broke as she asked the question.

"Does it really matter?" The man let out a low chuckle. "No, I'm not Rick Evermore, though he is—was—the real owner of this lovely piece of property. You couldn't pay me to live isolated like this."

The man pulled Tess closer against him. "If you'd just kept your mouth shut and not started snooping, we wouldn't be in this situation. But you couldn't do that could you?"

"I'm a sheriff's deputy," Kellan said. "What did you expect? But you knew that, and that's why you wanted us to stay, isn't it? You needed to know what information I have and why I was going to Shadow Ridge."

The man shrugged. "I want you to slowly put it on the ground."

As he followed the instructions, Kellan's mind raced to

come up with a way out of this. From the icy expression on the man's face, Kellan knew he wouldn't hesitate to kill them. There had to be a solution. He had to convince the man that they had what he needed.

Kellan took a step forward as he dug up the information from his memory. "Your real name is Aaron Manning, a traitor with the FBI who sold his soul for information on that drive."

The surprise on the man's face confirmed that Kellan was right on target.

Kellan held the other man's gaze. "What was your plan? To ambush them all out here in the desert?"

Manning's shoulders slumped. "We were the ones ambushed by a group of thugs who were after our supplies."

"Don't try to play the victim here," Kellan said, praying his strategy worked. "Let her go, and I'll tell you what I know about the flash drive."

Manning shook his head, still not ready to play ball. "Good try, but I still hold the cards here."

"Not all the cards." Kellan put on his best poker face while trying to avoid the terror in Tess's eyes. "You invited us in because you needed information. You need to know what I know about the flash drive. I know that you shot your partner, Lawrence Haley, along with the real Rick Evermore."

The man's jaw dropped just enough for Kellan to read his reaction.

"You were willing to torture your partner for that drive," Kellan rushed on, "and yet you're still here, so I'm guessing that whatever you did to those men to try and get information didn't work. You've been searching this property for that flash drive, but you still have no idea where it is, do you? But I spoke with Mac before he died. "

"Mac didn't have the flash drive. Lawrence did."

"Maybe." Kellan took another small step forward, knowing he needed to choose his words very carefully. "You really think they didn't suspect you were a mole?"

"They had no idea."

"I wouldn't bet my life on that if I were you. They had a plan to make sure you didn't get your hands on that drive."

"I don't believe you. You're trying to play me, but it won't work."

"And if I'm telling the truth? I told you I was on my way to Shadow Ridge with information, and you know I talked to Mac Hanna. He told me he didn't trust you and what their plan was if something went wrong."

Manning's frown deepened. "You're lying."

"Knowing both sides would kill for the information on it," Kellan continued, "I'm guessing you were planning to get paid very highly for it. Though I can't help but wonder if you still think it's worth it. Selling your soul rarely is. You had to kill both of them, and you still have no idea where the flash drive is."

Manning glanced up as storm clouds covered the remaining light of the moon. "I guess we're at a standoff. We both need what the other has, but I still don't trust you."

"Believe me, the feeling's mutual."

The wind was picking up. An empty plastic bucket tumbled across the yard between them before slamming against the outhouse.

"We both have another problem. None of us are going

anywhere." Manning nodded toward the house. "We'll go back inside and ride out this storm for now, but just know that if you try anything stupid—anything at all—I won't hesitate to kill your girlfriend."

CHAPTER THIRTEEN

Tess winced as Rick—Manning—tightened his grip on her arm and dragged her back inside the cabin. Her mind fought to process the conversation she'd just heard. The man who'd taken them in was some rogue FBI agent who'd killed his partners over a missing flash drive.

Manning sat them both down, then quickly secured them with zip ties to the wooden chairs. "Not that this probably needs to be said, but stay put. I'm going to grab some more wood off the porch, assuming that staying warm is the one thing we can all agree on."

A blast of cold air burst into the room as Manning went through the door.

Tess turned to Kellan. "Did my being shot at and drugged have anything to do with this?"

"I don't think so, but honestly. . .I don't know."

She tried to fight the panic as Manning returned with another gust of wind and an armload of chopped wood then somehow managed to kick the door shut behind him.

"The reason I was heading to Shadow Ridge," Kellan whispered, leaning forward, "was to find these men. Now, apparently he's the only one alive."

Tess worked to put the pieces together. "Do you really know where this flash drive is?"

"I'm just trying to keep us alive."

So he had been bluffing. But he had a point. They were still both alive. Now they just had to find a way to stay that way.

Manning dropped the wood into the rack, popped a couple of small logs into the woodstove, then turned around.

"I want you both to shut up," he said, dragging her chair to the other side of the room. "Stop talking."

Tess frowned at the order, fearful that this house of cards Kellan had created to protect them was about to all fall down. Once the storm passed, and he couldn't produce what the man wanted, they were going to be the next victims dumped into that grave. But there was one thing in their favor. Manning looked genuinely worried. She didn't know how much of what Kellan had told Manning was actually true, but it had been enough to create a storm cloud of doubts in his mind.

As for Kellan, she could read the frustration on his face. She'd noticed over the past two days how his jaw tensed and his brow furrowed when he was trying to solve a problem. She might not have known him for long, but at least she knew she could trust him. Even trust, though, wasn't enough to dissolve the anxiety pressing against her chest.

She could hear the wind whipping against the side of

the house and see through the window the light snow that continued to fall outside. Winter storms like this were rare, making her grateful they had shelter from the weather, but how long was this reprieve going to last?

Tess tugged on the zip tie digging into her wrists, wondering how a decision to rescue someone's cat had led her here. Even if they were able to overpower Manning, they were miles away from the nearest town, and the storm brewing outside showed no signs of stopping. She'd told Kellan how drawing the crime scene sketches for her brothers had affected her, but this situation had shifted everything. She was no longer the observer standing behind the sketchpad. She was now suddenly the victim, being held hostage by a murderer.

The sound of breaking glass jerked her from her thoughts. Wind whipped in from where a board from the shaded veranda had fallen and shattered the window. Within seconds, an icy blast of cold air filled the space.

"There's a roll of plastic in the far corner, and I saw a staple gun in the box of tools by the front door." Kellan jumped up, but his hands were still bound to the chair behind him. "I can help, but you're going to have to undo the zip tie—"

"Don't even think about it. Sit down."

With the temperature inside now dropping, Manning quickly grabbed the supplies. He shoved the fallen board back outside, broke off several large shards of glass, and started stapling the black plastic to the wooden frame.

"Are you sure you don't want my help?" Kellan asked as Manning fought to secure the plastic that was flapping in the wind.

"Very sure."

"You okay?" Kellan scooted his chair closer to Tess.

She was far from okay, and cold again from the icy wind, but she nodded anyway. Kellan had enough to worry about without her dumping her long list of fears on him.

Besides, there was another, more urgent, problem.

"There's a shard of glass from the window in your arm," she said. "You're bleeding."

Kellan glanced down at his arm. "Now I know what that pain was."

"It might need stitches—something I can't do—but it does need to be cleaned and bandaged." She turned to their captor, who was still busy securing the shattered window. "Manning. . .I need to take care of Kellan's arm. There's a first-aid kit in his backpack."

"I'm kind of busy," he said, tugging on the flapping plastic.

"Please, Manning."

Manning frowned, but a moment later he had his knife out of his pocket, and he quickly snapped off her zip tie. Grabbing Kellan's backpack, he dug around until he pulled out the first-aid kit. "Don't do anything stupid."

She rubbed her sore wrists, surprised he'd actually agreed to her request. She knew he was thinking there was nowhere for her to run, but they didn't need to run. They needed to find a way to overpower him and get control of the weapons he had on him.

How hard could that be?

Tess set the supplies on the counter, then quickly pulled out tweezers, antiseptic, antibiotic ointment, a couple of butterfly bandages, and a pair of medical scissors.

She bent down next to Kellan and whispered while

Manning went back to fixing the window. "I hope you have a plan."

"I always have a plan." He smiled up at her. "I just can't decide which one is best."

"Funny."

She carefully shoved the pair of scissors under Kellan's thigh, then held up the tweezers. "This is probably going to hurt."

"Can't hurt worse than it does right now."

She doused the site and the tweezers with antiseptic, then slowly pulled out the piece of glass.

"Ouch." Kellan's smile shifted into a grimace. "I guess it can hurt worse."

"It was deeper than I thought, but it's out. Hopefully all in one piece."

Manning stapled the last corner of the plastic to the window frame, then walked over to where she was working, apparently not trusting her to make good choices.

"Finished yet?" he asked.

"Not quite." Tess held up the shard. "Just patching him up."

"Give me the tweezers and finish up."

She opened up the first butterfly bandage while Manning paced.

What would her father do?

Before the Quake, he'd never been interested in technology and only used what was absolutely necessary for his job as a lawman. While his job had been rigorous at times, he'd still preferred the slower pace of Shadow Ridge to a bustling city. On top of that, he was also an expert marksman and master tracker who had taught her to prepare for the unexpected.

Well, this situation had definitely been unexpected.

So if her father *were* here, he'd be working on half a dozen plans.

"Finished?" Manning pressed.

"Almost." She secured the second butterfly bandage, then stepped back. "That should keep it from getting infected."

Manning pulled out another zip tie. "Sit back down."

"Just a sec." Tess dropped the ointment and antiseptic back in the first aid kit, stalling for time to come up with something while her hands were still untied.

She glanced at the black plastic that now covered the window. The real Rick Evermore would be prepared for any scenario. Bad weather. Water shortages. Unwanted intruders on his property. . .

That's it.

The wind had started to calm outside. All they needed was something to shift the odds in their favor.

"I need to go to the outhouse first," she said, snapping the lid to the first-aid kit shut and then setting the kit on the end of the bed.

Manning frowned.

"The wind has calmed down some," she rushed on, "and it's not as if I'm going to go anywhere. Not in the middle of this storm."

"Fine." He nodded toward the door. "But don't be gone long, or I'll come after you myself."

She grabbed her coat, slipped it on, then stopped at the door. "I'll need the flashlight."

Manning nodded at the table where the flashlight lay. She grabbed it, then hurried out into the cold. Icy wind whipped around her, making her momentarily second-guess her plan. She pulled her jacket tighter, realizing she didn't need the flashlight as the moon now shone against the snow and lit up the yard.

She stopped in front of the outhouse, hesitated for a moment, then went inside. She'd mentioned to Kellan how much she missed showers, but that wasn't the only thing she missed. After the Quake, most people had come up with either some sort of outdoor composting toilets or a long-drop system. Having a working, indoor bathroom would feel like the lap of luxury at this point. Running hot water, flushing toilets, a hot sudsy bath whenever she wanted. . .

She pushed aside the worthless fantasy, turned on the flashlight, then shut the door behind her. Her father kept handguns in several key locations on the ranch in case he needed a second firearm. Her grandfather had talked about keeping one in the outhouse. She didn't know anything about the real Rick Evermore, but he was a man who'd lived off the grid for a long time and had to be prepared for anything. Living this isolated, it only made sense that he would have made sure he had availability to a weapon at all times.

She shone the light along the wooden walls, searching for anything that might give a clue to a hiding place.

Nothing.

She swallowed her frustration and started searching higher, then stopped. One of the boards stuck out a quarter of an inch. Standing on the top of the toilet seat, she managed to pull up the loose board and there it was, hidden in a small hole. A Springfield HD pistol.

. . .

CHAPTER FOURTEEN

KELLAN WATCHED THE DOOR, waiting for Tess to return. The wind rippled against the black plastic covering the window, making slapping noises, but somehow it held. He was worried. He'd caught the look in Tess's eyes as she'd slipped outside. He had no idea what she was planning, but he was worried whatever it was might backfire. Not that he didn't think she was capable, but his bluff wasn't going to hold up much longer under Manning's scrutiny.

And once their leverage was gone, their time was up.

"I can see why you like her." Manning stood in front of the fire, watching the door. "She's a bit of a spitfire."

"She's just a friend."

"Keep telling yourself that. This is why you'll never excel at your job. You let your emotions get in the way. Your feelings for her have erased your common sense."

Kellan turned as the door flew open. Tess stepped through the doorway with a pistol aimed at Manning.

A split second later, Manning had his gun out of his holster and aimed at Kellan.

"I honestly didn't think you had it in you, but it doesn't matter," Manning said, holding his weapon steady as he moved closer to Kellan. "Drop the gun, or I'll shoot your boyfriend here."

"Okay, but here's the deal," Tess said, holding the pistol steady. "You shoot him, and I'll shoot you. And trust me when I say I know how to shoot."

"I say you're bluffing."

"Am I? My father is former Chief of Police Garrett McQuaid. I guess you don't know him, but Rick Evermore would have. He taught me how to shoot before I could drive a car. I have brothers, and I made it my goal to shoot as well or better than the three of them. And guess what, I can."

Tess pulled the trigger, hitting a glass inches from Manning's right hand. It shattered across the table, dripping water onto the floor.

"That wasn't a lucky shot," Tess said. "Drop the gun. Now."

Manning hesitated, giving Kellan the opening he needed. He stood up and swung his chair into the man's side as hard as he could. Manning's gun went off, hitting the ceiling and scattering dust and debris onto the floor below. Kellan struck the man again with the chair, and the gun flew out of his hand. Tess quickly picked it up then grabbed the medical scissors that had fallen to the floor. She snapped the binds off Kellan's wrists while he stood over Manning, his heel in the man's back.

"There are more zip ties in the left kitchen drawer," Kellan said.

She pulled some out, and handed them to him.

"We're going to make doubly sure you can't get away,"

Kellan said, securing both Manning's wrists and ankles, then anchoring him to the table leg.

Manning tugged, apparently still not ready to admit defeat. "You're going to end up regretting this."

"Somehow I don't think so," Kellan said.

"I should have gone with my gut." Manning's gaze shifted to Tess. "You never would have shot me."

"I guess we'll never know, will we?" Tess said.

Kellan made sure Manning wasn't going anywhere, then walked over to where Tess stood near the fire. "I'm impressed. You're definitely a McQuaid."

Tess still held the gun at her side, but she was shaking.

"Tess," he said, removing the weapon from her trembling hand. "Let me have the gun. Are you okay?"

"He's right. I don't think I could have shot him." She looked up at him wide-eyed. "Because if I had—"

"You didn't have to, and now it's over. And Manning. . .he's just trying to get into your head. You were amazing."

"Then why do I feel like I need to throw up?"

He pulled her trembling body into his arms and lowered his voice. "Just breathe, Tess. You're safe, and I'm going to get you home."

He felt the tension in her body start to melt as she pressed in against his chest. He kept his arms around her, watching for signs that her breathing and heart rate were slowing down.

"Where did you get the gun?" he asked.

She gave him the hint of a smile. "Like you said, I'm a McQuaid. My father taught me to be prepared for anything. I figured Rick would also be prepared. It was just a guess, but I thought he might have backup weapons around his property for an emergency. Like the outhouse. And thankfully for us, I was right."

"I'll trust your instincts any day," Kellan said.

"Like my instinct that he wouldn't shoot you," she whispered.

"I was right, wasn't I?" Manning's voice tried to push its way between them. "You've both been bluffing."

"Ignore him," Kellan said, pulling Tess closer and redirecting her attention to him. "Though I'm glad you were worried about me."

Apparently, his attempt at humor fell flat when her frown deepened.

"I don't know if any of this will ever be over," she said. "And if all of this was done as some kind of. . .terrorist attack. . . Do you know who's behind this?"

"Just a few sketchy details." Kellan lowered his voice. "The flash drive contains names of those involved in shutting down the grid and those who have infiltrated as double agents, along with intel pointing to where their base of operations is and other classified information."

"Sounds like something that could be devastating to either side. But who's behind this?"

Kellan tried unsuccessfully to ignore her nearness as he answered, "Some multinational, underground group. Clearly funded and well organized."

"To what end?"

"I don't know."

She glanced at Manning, who was still fuming. "What now?"

"I guess we still need to wait out the storm, but I'm ready to get you back to Shadow Ridge." He stepped back, then ran his hands up and down her arms. "Are you still cold?"

She nodded. "Yes, but better."

"Go sit by the fire."

"I want to sweep up the broken glass first."

"Okay, and in the meantime, I have a few questions for our traitor."

Kellan grabbed a chair, flipped it around, and sat down in front of Manning. "I think we've established that you stuck around because you believe the flash drive is here someplace."

Manning pressed his shoulders back. "You have no idea what you're talking about or what kind of hornet's nest you're poking at. If I were you I'd run as far away from here as possible and forget you ever got tangled up in this mess."

"One, I don't scare easily, and two, you're not the only one who wants to find that drive."

"It doesn't matter what you do," Manning said. "It doesn't matter if you find it or not. What's put into place can't be stopped. Not by you, not by anyone. And no matter what you do, you're insignificant. So you can threaten, coerce, drag me off to the salt mines...it won't matter. Someone else will take my place. And they will win."

"Noble words for someone who's just failed his one assignment," Kellan said, feeling as if he were hitting a brick wall. "Maybe you're right. Maybe you're wrong. I've found that those who have something worth fighting for can change history with the smallest of deeds. All it takes is people like Tess, willing to risk her life in a storm to search for something to save us. Like the man out in the grave who fought for his life, motivated by his loyalty to his country. Those are the people who will be remembered, not people like you."

Manning let out a low chuckle. "I was like you at one time, idealistic and principled, but that didn't get me anywhere. In this new world, you're going to want to be on the right side. Will there be casualties along the way? Yes. But in the long run their goal—"

"What is their goal?" Tess asked, holding a dustpan filled with glass. "Everything, as far as we know, is ruined. There is no infrastructure, no central government, no electricity or water. . . Are you really willing to sacrifice yourself for a plan where there's nothing left to fight for?"

Manning shook his head. "They have a plan to rebuild this country in ways you can't even imagine."

"Who are 'they'?" Tess insisted.

Manning's gaze shifted down, and Kellan caught what he'd been looking for.

"You're afraid," he said.

Manning laughed. "Of you?"

"No. Of whoever you're working for." Kellan held the man's gaze. "You assumed—wrongly—that getting that drive to them would set you up on the winning side. But you're nothing more than another pawn in this chess game."

"You have no idea what you're talking about."

"What happens if you don't get the flash drive?" Kellan asked. "I have a feeling you're as disposable to them as your partners were to you. If you don't produce the flash drive, they'll either think you're a traitor or worthless as an asset. Either way, I'm thinking once they track you down, without that flash drive, you're not worth anything to them and they'll get rid of you. And that's what you're afraid of. That someone will take your place. Because *you* are insignificant to them."

Manning squirmed in his chair, staring at the floor. "You don't know what you're talking about."

"Maybe not, but here's what I do know. I've traveled this entire county, and people are coming together to get their lives back. That's something you won't be able to stop. They're resilient, and whatever this. . .this takeover is. . .we're going to stop it. Good is going to win. Good has to win."

"Don't count on it. Like I said. I'm just a small piece of the puzzle. And despite what you think about me, I'm willing to sacrifice for the good of the whole."

"One more question," Kellan said, standing up. "When you tortured your partner for the location of the drive, did he give you any clues as to where he put it?"

"Why?"

"Humor me."

"He said if I killed him, I'd never find it." Manning's expression darkened. "Apparently, he was right."

CHAPTER FIFTEEN

TESS LEANED against the kitchen counter, trying not to imagine what agent Haley had gone through. She'd always avoided torture scenes in movies, but Manning talked about it as if he were the hero in the scenario.

But Aaron Manning was no hero.

She looked through the small window above the kitchen sink. The storm outside seemed to be abating, but everything that had happened over the past forty-eight hours had left her on edge, and she knew the only way to combat the rising anxiety was to do something. Finding the gun in the outhouse had helped. Made her feel as if she wasn't powerless against the enemy. She just wished there was a way to reverse the fate of the two men Manning had killed and buried outside.

Kellan came up to her. "Feeling any better?"

"It helps that he's the one tied to the chair." She forced a smile and started filling up the kettle with water. "I thought I'd make some coffee before we go. I don't know about you, but I could use a caffeine jolt."

"You could get a couple more hours of sleep before we leave," Kellan offered. "It looks like the storm is letting up—"

"There's no way I can sleep. I'll make some more coffee, and I saw some packages of oatmeal if you're hungry."

Kellan nodded, but from his expression, breakfast was the last thing on his mind.

"What about you?" She set the kettle on the stove, then turned back to him. "How are you doing?"

"I'm frustrated," he said, keeping his voice low. "I feel like we've got nothing. I can't get anything out of Manning. I know the general direction to Shadow Ridge, but with this storm, it's still a risk. And yet staying here. . ." He glanced at Manning than back to her. "Let's just say, it's moments like this that I really wish I could call for backup."

She rested her hand on his arm. "We'll figure this out. We have to."

"We'll have to take Manning with us, and as for the two men he killed. . .I want to make sure they're properly buried so their bodies aren't dug up by wild animals."

She grabbed the oatmeal packets she'd seen earlier along with three bowls, understanding all too well his frustrations. Sometimes it felt like no matter how hard they tried, evil always won. So many suffered loss and continued to struggle on a daily basis. All because of the selfish desires of others.

She pulled open a drawer, looking for the silverware, then stopped. A thin stack of papers was folded and wedged in the back of the drawer. How had she missed them?

"Kellan. . .I might have something." She started flipping through them, stopping at a detailed map.

Bingo.

Kellan stepped up next to her. "What is it?"

"It says it's a certified survey map of this property from the county."

"This is exactly what we need." He shone his flashlight on the black-and-white drawing. "It shows the property lines, but includes enough additional data that we should be able to use it to get us to Shadow Ridge."

Tess stifled the urge to fly into his arms, needing that extra reassurance that he was right. They still had to deal with Manning, but maybe they'd just found a way out of this nightmare.

"I'll have the coffee ready in about five minutes. We can gather up our stuff and go."

"There's a wagon in the barn," Kellan said, rolling up the map and dropping it into his backpack. "I think we need to round up food and other supplies and take them with us."

She knew he was right, but the idea still bothered her. "Doesn't that seem wrong?"

"I'd much rather the items end up in the hands of people who really need them, than a bunch of thieves who would just turn around and sell them on the black market for profit."

"The two of you think you have all this figured out, don't you?" Manning's voice broke into their discussion. "You think you can fix this situation with a jolt of caffeine and a map while you check off your do-gooder list."

"Shut up, Manning."

The veins in Kellan's neck pulsed, his irritation clearly growing.

"I'll start gathering the supplies, if you want to go get the wagon set up," she said.

"Forget it. I'm not leaving you alone with him. There are some wooden crates stacked up on the side of the porch. I'll help you fill them."

Fifteen minutes later, they'd filled four crates with usable items, mainly from the kitchen, and downed mugs of bitter coffee, forgoing the oatmeal. Apparently, she wasn't the only one who'd lost her appetite.

Tess looked around the small space, then went to grab the first-aid kit she'd left on the bed. Her shoe crunched on something. She reached down and pulled a jagged piece of glass from the sole of her shoe, grateful she wasn't barefoot. She must have missed some of the glass when she swept it up.

Tess glanced up at the window, the black plastic still fluttering in the wind, and froze.

A memory surfaced.

The mayor had told her that there were armed riders outside the house. She'd heard a shot. The mayor had told her to stay down. She hadn't seen whoever had been out there, but when she'd followed the mayor out the door she'd glanced back into the living room. The window had been shot out. She'd seen that. But the nagging question in the back of her mind finally surfaced. There'd been no glass on the table beneath the window.

Tess stared at the shard of glass in the palm of her hand as the eerie realization took hold. The window in Walter's house hadn't been shot at from the outside—it had been shot at from the inside. Which meant the mayor must have done it.

But why?

She closed her eyes. Maybe her memories were still jumbled. Why would the mayor lie to her, creating a situation that never happened? It didn't make sense. What made more sense was that the drug had altered her memory, leaving holes in it that hadn't returned.

And yet. . .

She turned back to Kellan. "There was no glass."

Kellan frowned. "What do you mean?"

"The mayor told me that someone had shot at the front window of Walter's place. It was why we ran out the back way. I never saw anyone, but I did see the broken window. There should have been glass on the table if someone had shot at it from outside the house."

Her mind worked to unravel the facts as she knew them, but it still didn't make sense. There was no obvious reason for the mayor to lie to her, but it was the only explanation she could think of.

"What are you saying, Tess? You think the mayor was behind your being drugged. . .behind Walter's death?"

"It seems crazy, but yes."

But still. . .

She'd never noticed any red flags. Mayor Shannon might come across as somewhat eccentric with his bow ties and plaid suit jackets, but other than that, he seemed to be well liked by the town. So why would he have lied about the window being shot at unless he was trying to cover up something?

On top of that, she'd never seen anyone else, not even

when she'd gone with him into the woods. The last thing she remembered was him standing near her. Could he have injected her with something? The whole scenario seemed ridiculous. There had to be a connection. . .like Walter's notebook?

What if she *was* right? What if it was the mayor who drugged her and then shot at them. Like Walter, she had to have stumbled onto something, but what?

She caught Kellan's gaze. "Why did the mayor want me to think there were people out there?"

"With the limited facts we have, I have no idea."

"There has to be a connection to Walter's notebook."

Her chest tightened. Panic pressed hard against her sternum. Walter died of arsenic poisoning. She was almost sure of that. But what was the mayor trying to hide? He said he was waiting for Jace, which had made sense, but he had to have had a reason to make up the outside shooters.

Her mind spun in circles. If the mayor had lied to her about that, what else had he lied about?

"Tess—"

She tossed the piece of glass into the trash. "It doesn't matter. Not right now. We need to concentrate on getting to Shadow Ridge."

She couldn't let her mind go off on some tangent. She needed to stay focused on the here and now. Whatever had happened back at Walter's house, there was nothing she could do about it until she got back to Shadow Ridge.

Kellan stopped in front of her and pressed his hands on her shoulders. "This does matter."

"You think there's a connection with everything that's happened here?" she asked.

"It doesn't seem likely, but finding out who drugged and shot at you is just as important as this situation. What are you thinking?"

She glanced where Manning sat on the other side of the room, wishing she didn't feel as if the man's beady eyes were studying her.

"Okay." She forced her mind to rearrange the pieces, needing a clearer picture. "Our theory was that Walter found out something he shouldn't have, possibly the murder of the Palmers that someone tried to cover up as arsenic poisoning."

"We still need evidence, but it's definitely plausible."

Tess nodded. "Walter was using a filter system, one we believe worked, and yet his body showed signs of arsenic poisoning."

"So whoever murdered him might not have known he was using a filter, and wouldn't know that his death from arsenic poisoning would be questioned."

"Kellan, if I'm right, the mayor could be behind at least three deaths."

Had the person who'd killed Walter been with her that whole time? Been someone she'd trusted?

How had she missed that?

"Tess. . ."

"The mayor was with me in Walter's house, Kellan. He drugged me and left me to die. If you hadn't found me. . ."

He squeezed her shoulders then dropped his hands to his sides. "But I did find you, and you're okay. I'm going to get you back to Shadow Ridge so we can find the truth. And in the meantime, I'm not going to let anyone hurt you."

She nodded, grateful he'd rescued her and had been able to keep her safe. Now she needed to get control of her fear and trust that he'd get her back to Shadow Ridge.

"I'll be okay." She tugged on the hem of her shirt. "I just hate that he was right there with me that whole time and I had no idea what he was doing."

"You ready to go?" Kellan asked.

"Yeah. I think we've got everything except Manning."

Kellan started for their prisoner, then stopped.

"Did you forget something?" she asked.

"Haley told Manning he'd never find the flash drive, *if* he were dead. What if that statement wasn't just an empty threat?"

"Wait a minute." She shook her head. "I'm not following."

"Sorry. You said the mayor was with you the entire time, and it triggered something." Kellan motioned for her to go outside with him, but left the door open so he could still keep an eye on Manning. "What if Lawrence Haley had the drive the entire time?"

"It seems unlikely that Manning would have missed that."

"Agreed. But what if Haley swallowed it?"

"Okay. Wow. That's not what I was expecting." Tess's eyes widened. "It seems a bit far-fetched. He could've smashed it if he wanted to destroy it, but swallow it?"

"Think about it. It was probably a split-second decision, and the only way he could ensure the other side didn't get the information on it."

The theory seemed ridiculous, yet…"I suppose it's possible, but how are you going to prove it?"

"We're going to have to get the body back to Shadow Ridge and have your sister do an autopsy."

CHAPTER SIXTEEN

KELLAN NAVIGATED the wagon down the narrow trail, grateful that the skies had finally cleared. The recent storm had left behind a covering of snow on the ground, creating a rare winter scene that had frosted the distant mountains as well as the surrounding terrain. In another couple of hours, he'd have Tess back to her family and all of this would be over.

At least that part of his undertaking would be over.

Manning walked in front of the wagon, secured with a zip tie plus a rope Kellan had found in the barn that he'd attached to the wagon. Letting this former agent escape wasn't an option. He glanced back at Haley's body, covered in black plastic and nestled between the supplies they'd packed in the wagon. A tragic and unnecessary ending to a man's life as far as he was concerned. A man who'd died nobly trying to help save his country. The only upside in the last couple of days was the woman sitting next to him on the wooden bench.

Tess McQuaid had been the unexpected wildcard in

the equation, but the more time he spent with her, the more impressed he was with her spot-on instincts, kind heart, and staunch courage.

"I bet if someone had told you a year ago that you'd be driving a horse and wagon to Shadow Ridge," Tess said, shifting his thoughts, "you'd have laughed in their face."

He glanced at her bundled up in her pink coat and knitted beanie with a look of amusement on her face. Somewhere in the middle of everything that had happened, he'd completely fallen for her. No. He pushed aside the distracting thoughts, needing to focus on getting them to Shadow Ridge in one piece.

Kellan cleared his throat. "Not exactly the same as the V8 engine and hellcat widebody I used to drive."

"No, but I'll admit there's something to slowing down and taking the slower path. Makes me wish I had my sketchbook with me. It's been a while since I've seen snow, and this winter wonderland with its snowy cacti, frozen desert scrub, and icy spider webs. . ."

"Your artist eye," he said, loving her ability to see beauty in the simple things. "I'd still love to see some of your drawings."

A slight blush crossed her cheeks. "Maybe one day."

The wagon jostled beneath them as they crossed a rough part of the trail.

"Sorry," he said.

"Forget it. This beats walking, but it also makes me feel slightly sorry for our prisoner," Tess said. "He looks like he's worn out."

Like Hugo and Camden, the feuding neighbors, Kellan held little sympathy toward the man who'd betrayed both his partners and his country.

"I don't. We can't take any chances of him getting away, and if this is what it takes, then I don't mind a bit of cruel and unusual punishment. He tortured his last victim. Walking to Shadow Ridge in front of us is nothing."

Kellan glanced at her, hating the fact that the past year had hardened him. The daily challenge of bringing justice to a world that had fallen apart had brought him face-to-face with situations that, even as an officer of the law, he'd never thought he'd have to deal with. Men like Aaron Manning who'd betrayed his country.

Still. . .

"That sounded completely heartless, I know," he said.

"Maybe a little, but you're right." Her hands gripped the wooden bench of the wagon as they jostled over another rut. "I guess I just can't help but think how all of this was so unnecessary. Two more people are dead, and why? Because of someone else's selfishness."

"That does seem like the common denominator."

She glanced at him. "So do you get frustrated with people's decisions, or have you been doing this long enough that you just accept it?"

Kellan let out a low chuckle. "The day before I found you, I was breaking up a fight between two grown men. One had tied the other up for allegedly stealing his chickens. It wasn't the first time we'd been called out to their properties, and if I'm honest, it frustrates me every single time."

"Chickens?" Her eyes widened. "What did you do?"

"Told them I was going to lock them both up in the same jail cell until they sorted out their differences. Out of all the things we deal with on a daily basis, calls like that just make me angry. With limited resources, refereeing a chicken spat is a complete waste of time."

"I'm sure my brothers have some of the same stories. I get it, because you face enough real crises every day."

"I guess the reality is that nothing has really changed. The situations might have shifted when the grid went down, but we're still dealing with selfishness."

Tess stared out at the trees that seemed like they were suspended in a frozen fog. "I'll be honest, I struggle with where God is in all of this. I know it's easy to question Him when things go wrong. Why do we suddenly expect Him to fix everything?"

He was surprised at her candidness, but on the other hand, that was one of the things he liked about her.

"I've started to realize over the past few months that sometimes the smaller things are harder," she continued. "I find myself getting irritated about the little things. Until I'm just angry at everybody."

"I used to get angry about my father being in prison," Kellan said, understanding exactly where she was coming from. "Questioning why God would've allowed that to happen when I needed a father. Sometimes I'm still angry about it. Why couldn't God have done something, or sent somebody into his life to stop him?"

"That had to have been so hard for you to understand, especially as a kid."

"I'll be honest, I feel a little jealous of you and your relationship with your father," Kellan said as they rounded another bend and the terrain started to open up. "My father wasn't exactly the greatest example. Definitely not someone I strive to be like, and it's colored my view of a heavenly Father."

"Like how a good father could allow something like this to happen," she said.

"I feel a bit sacrilegious even thinking that, but yes. A good father wants what's best for his children, and I know that doesn't mean making everything easy for them, but I look around me and see people hurting every day." He paused, trying to clarify what he was saying. "I understand that God gave man free will, but when that choice affects others—Manning's a great example—it's hard."

"Hard and unfair, but God's been teaching me that His grace is so much bigger. Seeing the unfair only highlights that grace."

"It's still not easy."

She shook her head. "It isn't, but if you think about what happened on the cross. . .none of that was fair. Jesus was the innocent Son of God, and His response was still to redeem us."

"Wow." Kellan blew out a sharp breath. "Art isn't the only thing you're able to see with different eyes. I've never thought about it that way."

"It's actually something my father shared with me before the Quake, but I've never forgotten it. And yes, it is a struggle."

Here was another thing he liked about her. The ability to say what she thought without worry of judgment. The way she challenged him and made him realize it was okay to question the parts of his faith he struggled with.

"I recognize that slope topped with ponderosa pines," Tess said.

"I do too." Kellan breathed out a sigh of relief. "We should be in Shadow Ridge within the hour."

"I don't think I've ever looked so forward to one of Margaret's meals."

"She's the woman who lives with your family?"

Tess grabbed on to the side of the wagon as they went over another rut in the path. "She's become like a second mother to me. I don't know what I would've done without her. She's a nurse, so she was able to help my father with a lot of his physical therapy after he was shot. But now. . . Now she's just part of the family."

The narrow trail they were following turned until it was running parallel to a sharp drop-off on the right, and on the left, a scattered row of trees and stumps.

Manning turned around. "I'm getting tired."

"Keep walking, Manning," Kellan said.

Tess let out a sharp breath. "Be careful. The path gets close to the edge of the ravine, and I don't think it was meant for wagons."

Manning stopped for a moment while the horses kept going, allowing for slack in the rope connecting him to the wagon.

"Keep moving, Manning," Kellan shouted.

Manning took another step, then looped around one of the tree stumps on the side of the trail, halting their movement.

Manning started yelling at the horses, who bolted forward, pulling the rope taut again.

"He just snapped his zip tie, and he's trying to cut the rope with something," Tess said.

Which meant the only thing keeping them from going over the edge was the rope Kellan had secured around the man's wrists.

"Manning. . ." Kellan reached for his weapon as the horses reared in front of them.

The front wheel of the wagon slipped over the edge of the ridge, while all the supplies they'd packed in the back of the wagon shifted toward the edge, along with the dead body. If he didn't calm down the horses, they were all going over.

"Kellan!"

"Hang on, Tess."

Kellan fought to control the horses, but they were too agitated.

Another jolt knocked Tess from her seat and over the edge of the wagon. Her feet scrambled to find solid ground at the steep edge of the ravine. She managed to grab on to a metal rail of the wagon, but how much longer was she going to be able to hold on?

"Still feeling in control, Deputy?" Manning shouted.

The rope wrapped around the fat stump was keeping the wagon from going over, but if Manning managed to cut the rope, then they'd no longer be anchored to the stump.

"Grab my hand, Tess."

Kellan leaned over as far as he could. If he moved to the other side of the bench where it was easier to reach her, his weight could tip the wagon over the edge.

"I can't let go, or I'll fall."

He glanced down the steep ravine to his right. The slope was steeper than the one they'd fallen down. Rocks fell off the side as the wagon wheel slipped another couple of inches.

"You thought you could outsmart me, didn't you? But in another few seconds, you're going over the side. Judging from the angle and depth of that ravine, I'm pretty sure you won't survive the fall."

"Manning—"

"Begging doesn't look good on you, Deputy."

Anger shot through Kellan, but there wasn't time to react. He had to get to Tess before she fell, and he had to do it without tipping the wagon over.

"Kellan, I can't hold on."

"Yes, you can. Just a few more seconds."

They hadn't survived the past forty-eight hours to have things end this way. The wagon slid another inch toward the edge of the cliff, but he managed to grab Tess's hand.

"Hang on, Tess. Just a little longer. You can do this. I've got you."

He pulled with all his strength while she tried to get her feet back on the floor of the wagon. But there wasn't time. A gunshot sliced through the air as Tess's fingers slipped from Kellan's.

CHAPTER SEVENTEEN

TESS LOST her grip on Kellan's hand as the sound of a gunshot rippled through the air followed by men shouting. One second, she was slipping, the next, the wagon had righted, and she managed to find a place for her foot so she could hold herself up. Shouts continued around her while someone pulled her back up into the wagon. Her arms fell limp above her head as she lay on her stomach on the bench, trying to catch her breath. She had no idea what had happened, except that she was still alive and not at the bottom of the ravine.

"Tess. . . Tess, are you okay?"

"Daddy?"

Her father's voice thundered above the commotion. He swooped her into his arms and carried her off of the wagon, away from the edge of the ridge, then set her down gently onto the ground.

Her father's firm hands squeezed her shoulders as he looked her over. "Please tell me you're okay."

She wrapped her arms around his neck. "I am now."

"We've spent the last two days looking for you," he said. "I've been so worried."

"I know, and I'm sorry." She leaned back and searched his familiar, tanned face with its hint of a white beard, and tried to slow her breathing. "Where's Kellan?"

"Kellan?" her father asked.

She turned back toward the wagon where Jace had just handcuffed Manning and was talking to the rest of the search team. "Deputy Gray from Van Horn. He's the reason I'm alive."

"Tess." Kellan ran up to them.

Her father reached out and shook the deputy's hand. "I don't know exactly what went on, but it looks like I owe you my gratitude, son, for taking care of my daughter."

"I'm just thankful I found her, but your timing couldn't have been better."

Ranger, nuzzled up against her leg.

"Boy, I've missed you, buddy." Tess bent down and buried her face in Ranger's neck, trying to hold back the tears. This could have ended so differently. "I always told them I was your favorite. I was right, wasn't I?"

"I'm still trying to put the pieces together," her father said. "The mayor told us about the attack at Walter's house, that they chased after you and that someone knocked you both out. When he woke up, you and your horse were gone."

"I was on my way to Shadow Ridge and found your daughter," Kellan said.

"Tess McQuaid. . ."

Tess stood up as Mayor Shannon walked up to them. "Mayor? I didn't know you were here."

"You don't know how happy I am to see you alive and

well." He adjusted his glasses on the bridge of his nose and smiled. "When I woke up and you were gone. . . I didn't know what to think. I've been so upset, I insisted on joining the search party."

"Thankfully, I'm fine," Tess said. "Deputy Gray from Van Horn found me."

She tried to read the mayor's expression. She had no way to conclusively prove her theory. The mayor had been a viable part of the community the past year, and even though she knew he had some bad blood with her father, nothing that she knew of had gotten in the way of doing his job. But while she didn't want to think that the mayor was behind this, she still couldn't discount the broken glass.

There had to be a way to find out the truth.

"So what do you remember?" the mayor asked, tugging on his leather gloves.

"Whatever that drug was, it left holes in my memory," she said. "There are still a few blank spots. Things that I'm hoping I'll remember."

"I thought your memories had all come back," Kellan said.

Tess pressed her fingernails into his wrist. "For the most part, they have. But I still feel like I'm missing something important. Like there are still memories lingering in the shadows."

"We can talk about this later," her father said, ending the conversation. "My daughter's tired, and I just want to get her home."

"Of course," the mayor said. "I'll go set off the flare and get the other teams heading back to town."

Kellan pulled Tess aside while the mayor walked away. "What are you doing?"

"Trying to find out the truth," she said, keeping her voice low.

"And if there is any truth at all to your theory about the mayor's involvement, you just set yourself up. You don't think he'll try and get rid of another loose end? He's done it before."

"That was the point—"

"Is everything okay?"

Tess turned back to her father. "For now. We can talk more when we get back to town. You're right. I'm tired."

"We have your prisoner secure," Jace said, stepping up and pulling Tess into a tight hug. "I'm glad you're okay, Sis."

"Me too."

Her father rubbed the back of his neck. "Who is your prisoner?"

"Long story short, he's an FBI agent, Aaron Manning, who decided to turn against his country for profit," Kellan said.

"And almost killed the two of you from the looks of it," Jace said.

"You think this Manning is connected to Tess's abduction?" her father asked.

"Not that we know of," Kellan said.

"Thanks for showing up when you did." Tess squeezed her father's hand. "But as much as I've been looking forward to getting home, we need to get to the clinic. We have a body in the back of the wagon we need Hope to autopsy."

Jace took a step back. "There's a body in the back of the wagon?"

"It's all connected to why I was on my way to Shadow Ridge," Kellan said. "The day before I left Van Horn, we pulled a man out of an old mineshaft. He was FBI, traveling with information on the grid going down, and he'd been shot. His security team had been killed in an ambush, and the other two agents he was with were missing."

"Information on the grid going down," her father said. "That's quite a development."

"Lawrence Haley turned out to be one of the missing agents, and I think it's possible that he swallowed the flash drive to keep the information from Manning."

"What's on the drive?" Jace asked.

"A list of moles within the Realm as well as other crucial information that needed to be taken to the capital."

"Looks like we really do have a lot of catching up to do," her father said. "What is the Realm?"

"An organized group that took down the grid and destroyed everything we know."

"They've done a pretty good job with that." Her father shook his head. "Let's go ahead and get back to Shadow Ridge. We can sort out everything there. And Kellan. . . You're welcome to stay at the ranch in the meantime."

"Thank you. I could certainly use a good night's sleep without worrying that someone is going to shoot us."

———

AN HOUR AND A HALF LATER, Tess stepped inside the lobby of the Shadow Ridge Police Station with her father,

Jace, and Kellan after leaving Lawrence Haley's body with Hope at the clinic. She stopped next to her father who had yet to leave her side, but with the mayor's presence, they hadn't had a chance to talk in private.

"I just need a few minutes to get your prisoner secured, and then we'll get you and Dad home, Tess," Jace said. "Levi's bringing Manning around to the back entrance right now."

"I need to talk to you both about Walter first," Tess said, unwilling to put off the conversation any longer. If the mayor was behind this, they had to find a way to prove it.

"Can it wait until later?" her father asked. "Jace is right. We need to get you home."

"I think you should hear her out, sir," Kellan said.

Tess caught the frown on Kellan's face and realized he was still irritated at her recklessness.

"Okay." Her father placed his hands on his hips. "What's going on?"

"I don't believe the mayor is telling the truth," she started. "I didn't see the people who shot at Walter's house, and I didn't see whoever drugged me, but I don't think it was some local thieves. Someone shot from inside the house. That's why there was no broken glass on the table below the window."

Her father glanced at Jace, then leaned against the edge of the empty reception desk. "I'm still not following."

"The shot came from inside the house," she said.

"You think the mayor shot out the window?" her father asked.

Tess nodded.

"Why?" Jace asked.

"I think he killed Walter in order to cover up another murder. Two murders, actually."

"That's a serious accusation," Jace said.

"I realize that, but I also have this notebook with Walter's notes." She pulled it out of her pocket and held it up. "I believe Walter was investigating the death of his neighbors, Jared and Raelynn Palmer."

"I thought they died from arsenic poisoning," her father said.

"They did."

"What exactly are you saying, Tess?" Jace asked.

"I believe the mayor killed them, and then killed Walter to cover up his tracks," she said. "I need to show you something else in Jace's office."

She walked into the small room that was furnished simply with a desk and a few chairs and file cabinets and stopped in front of the map on the far wall that had been marked with red dots to show the locations of the people who'd been affected or died from arsenic poisoning.

"Most of the poisoning happened northwest of the town in this area here," she said, pointing to the map.

Jace nodded. "There are two possible water sources we believe are tainted on that side of town."

Tess handed the notebook to her brother. "According to his notes, Walter believed that someone was using arsenic to cover up murder. A couple of weeks ago, he mentioned a feud between some of his neighbors. At the time I wasn't sure what it was. But it has to be this."

This time she tapped the Palmers' property. "There's a stream that flows from the Palmers' property to the adjoining property. If you look at this map, you can see whose property it flows to."

"The mayor's," Jace said.

"I believe the argument was about water rights," Tess continued. "It's happened before. Someone decides to dam up the water—"

"Essentially taking away the other person's water source," Kellan said.

"If I'm following correctly," Tess's father said, "which I think I am, then this is still just circumstantial evidence. Do you have proof besides a broken window, notes on a pad, and water-rights theories?"

"I'm going to get the mayor to confess."

"Tess. . ." Her father shook his head. "I don't like where this is heading."

"The mayor believes that there are pieces of my memory still missing. And that they're slowly coming back. He can't let me figure out what happened. That's what he was afraid of in the first place and why he drugged me. He couldn't take a chance that Walter had talked to me about his investigation."

"Okay, now I really don't like where this is going," her father said.

"If I'm right, he's killed three people, and apparently covering up what he did is not a problem. We can't let him get away with this."

"I'm not putting my daughter out as bait."

"Then we come up with a scenario where he confesses, and all of you come to my rescue."

CHAPTER EIGHTEEN

WITH RANGER BY HER SIDE, Tess stepped onto the porch of her sister's adobe house that sat just off Main Street, then turned to Kellan, who had escorted her from the police station. "Stop worrying. I'll be fine here while you help my father deal with Manning. It's important."

"I know. I just. . .I want you to be safe. I need you to be safe."

He held her gaze for a moment, stirring up another flood of emotions. She knew that becoming involved with Kellan would be a mistake, but she was having a hard time convincing her heart.

"I'll be fine," she said, softening her voice. "Thank you for everything, Kellan. I really do appreciate it."

He shot her a smile then headed back toward the station.

Ranger followed Tess into Hope's cozy living room filled with colorful throw pillows and candles. "Looks like it's just you and me, boy."

Spending the last year near her sister had been an

unexpected blessing of being stuck in Shadow Ridge. It had been a bonding time, giving her someone to both grieve with and laugh with. She walked over to the red brick fireplace and picked up a framed photo of Hope and Chase that had been taken before the Quake.

She'd been honest when she'd told Kellan about what she'd learned about God's grace and her changed perspective on life even when it seemed unfair. But it was still hard. Loss wasn't an equation to be solved. It was a crying out for answers and a physical heaviness against her chest that kept her up at night when all she wanted to do was escape reality.

Kellan understood that pain.

God understood that pain.

A knock shifted her attention to the front door. Her heart raced as a rush of adrenaline released.

She signaled for Ranger to sit, then opened the door. "Mayor. . . Is everything okay?"

"Yes, I just. . . I wanted to check on you." He glanced past her shoulder. "Can we talk? Just for a moment."

She hesitated, then let him inside before shutting the door behind him.

The mayor smiled. "I feel like I need to apologize. I should have gotten you to safety, and instead—"

"I don't blame you."

"So have you remembered anything else?"

"No, but I have a nagging feeling. You know. The feeling when you should remember something, but can't. It's frustrating, but I'm sure it will come back."

"There's been a lot of loss. I know you were friends with Walter."

"I was, and that's what's been bothering me, actually.

He was using one of the water filters, so I don't understand how he was poisoned."

"The filter must not have been working."

"I remember something." She caught and held his gaze. "Walter told me he was investigating something to do with the water. Death. A cover-up. Murder."

"Murder?"

"Murders. The Palmers. You killed them, didn't you?"

He shoved his glasses up the bridge of his nose, then shook his head. "I was hoping you didn't know anything, but you McQuaids have the bad habit of getting in the way."

Tess pressed her shoulders back, trying to keep the fear at bay. "Like Walter?" Ranger sat up next to her, but Tess motioned for him to stay. "You killed the Palmers, then covered up Walter's murder with arsenic poisoning."

Any friendliness left in the mayor's expression vanished. "He was nosy, though not as bad as the Palmers. They gave me no choice, really. They dammed the stream that ran from their property into mine, claiming they didn't have enough to share, but that left me with no water. I couldn't survive without water."

"Why didn't you just go to the police?"

"Let's just say they knew things about me, and now you know too much as well." The mayor shifted his stance. "The problem is, I really don't like messes, so here's what's going to happen."

Tess kept her gaze steady. "You're going to poison me too?"

"I learned a lot as a welder. You'd be surprised about the dangers in the welding business and the harmful fumes and gas byproducts that can be released. Lead, beryllium, argon, and even arsenic."

"I'm guessing you found a way to poison Walter's food, making it look like his water filter wasn't working and he died of arsenic poisoning. That mouse had the same fate."

"I was afraid it was just a matter of time until you figured it out. I just couldn't have expected that deputy to come to your rescue."

"You really did plan for me to die out there." Tess felt a shiver run through her. "Were you the one who shot at us?"

"You're too smart for your own good," the mayor said, drawing his weapon. "Just like your father."

"Ranger! *Fass!*"

Before the mayor could react, Ranger crossed the space, grabbed his arm, and pulled him to the ground. A second later, her father and brothers burst into the living room from the hallway, along with Kellan, where they'd been waiting.

Her father barked an order at Ranger to move back.

"This isn't going to end well for you, Mayor Shannon," Jace said, unloading the man's weapon.

Her father pulled her into a hug, then took a step back. "Are you okay?"

"A little unnerved—okay a lot unnerved—but I'm fine." She brushed a strand of hair out of her face, wishing she could take a long hot shower after the past couple of days. "I'm just grateful this is all behind us."

Her father glared at her brothers and Kellan. "I still can't believe the three of you talked me into sending your little sister into a sting situation."

"If you hadn't noticed, our little sister has grown up," Levi said.

"Interested in joining the force?" Jace asked.

Tess laughed. "Not a chance. And hopefully this will be the last time I have to help you with an investigation."

"I'm glad to hear that, but Tess. . .you were amazing." Tears filled her father's eyes as he pulled her into a hug. "Not that I ever doubted you. You look so much like your mother. She'd be so proud of you. I'm proud of you."

"I appreciate that," she said, hugging him back. "I'd also really like to go home now."

"Absolutely."

Kellan stepped forward. "I'd be happy to escort her."

Her father shot Kellan a guarded look. "I'm sure you would, but I need you back at the station. Shannon isn't the only felon we're dealing with."

"Yes, sir. Of course."

"LEVI," her father said. "Take your sister home, then meet us back at the station."

Ten minutes later, they'd saddled up a horse for Tess, and she was headed back to the family ranch with Levi.

"I guess Sugar never returned," she said as a cold wind whipped around her.

"I'm sorry. No. It's still possible she'll show up."

"I doubt it. Horses are worth too much, and there are horse thieves everywhere."

She tried to brush away the frustration. At least she—and Kellan—were alive. That was all that mattered right now.

"Tell me about you and Kellan," her brother probed.

"There's nothing to tell."

"Oh, come on. I saw the way he looked at you. That boy's smitten."

"How's Ava?" she questioned back.

"Don't change the subject."

She shot her brother a smile. "All's fair in love and war."

"Sometimes, little sister, you're too smart for your own good."

"I try." She laughed, but the smile quickly faded. "Kellan doesn't live in Shadow Ridge, so even if I was interested—and I'm not saying I am—it wouldn't work."

"There are ways around obstacles if you really want something."

"Like with Ava?"

Levi laughed. "Yes. I've completely fallen for the woman."

"I can't believe that I'm about to have two sisters-in-law."

"Let's not jump the gun quite yet, though I have a feeling that Jace and Morgan will be walking down the aisle soon."

"Why wait?" Tess asked. "The two of you seem happy."

"We are. Very. I guess I'm still pinching myself to make sure it's real and she's sticking around."

"I'm pretty sure Ava has no plans to go anywhere." Tess let out a low chuckle. "Even if she could."

They road past Crowley's Point, a crossroad not far from the entrance of the McQuaid ranch. Snowcapped mountains rose in the distance, framing the stunning view.

"By the way," Levi said, "Ava is extremely grateful that you've taken her sister under your wing. Having a friend around after what happened last month has really helped Josie."

"I know what it's like to feel out of the loop, and besides, she's pretty cool. She's teaching me how to use the longboard, and I've promised to give her some art lessons. She's wanting to learn anime, which is a bit out of my skillset, but I think I can help her with the basics."

"I'm just glad you're okay," Levi said. "And Tess. . .don't dismiss Kellan too quickly. Things have a way of working out. From what I've seen, he'd be a pretty good catch, though he'd still be getting the better end of the deal."

CHAPTER NINETEEN

TESS TOOK a sip of the spicy chai tea she'd been drinking, then sat back in her sister's cushioned dining room chair. She tried to have lunch with Hope at least once a week, and today, she'd brought some of Margaret's homemade carrot soup with her. She hadn't seen much of Kellan or her father or brothers over the past few days. They'd all been busy dealing with the fallout from Walter's death and the arrest of Aaron Manning and the mayor.

While Manning had continued to remain silent, Hope had found the flash drive in Lawrence Haley's stomach contents during the autopsy. Now it was a matter of finding out if his stomach acid had corroded the data on the drive, or if it was possible to retrieve it. Jace and Kellan were working on recovering the files, using a solar panel for power.

The mayor had been arrested, not only for the three more serious charges of murder, but also for the embezzlement of city funds over the past four years, something the Palmers, apparently, had been holding over him.

Tess glanced at the cloudless sky through the open window.

"Do you have plans this afternoon?" Hope asked, taking her time with her tea. "You seem. . .antsy."

Tess took another sip. "I'm going out for a little bit."

"Alone?"

"No." Tess had prepared herself for a string of questions when Hope hadn't left to go back to the clinic when she normally did. "Kellan's coming by. He wants to show me something in town."

"Ahh. . ." Hope's smile widened. "Deputy Gray probably wants to show you the mistletoe the holiday committee has been hanging along Main Street for Christmas."

"Please. That's why I didn't tell you I was going out," Tess said, trying to convey with the tone of her voice that seeing Kellan was no big deal. "It's not a date. We're just going for a walk. He's heading back to Van Horn tomorrow, and he wanted to say goodbye."

Hope got up from the table and went to rinse out her mug. "I didn't think they'd recovered the data on the drive yet."

"They haven't, but Kellan needs to get back in order to give the sheriff an update. He's been gone almost a week now."

"I'm guessing he'll be back in Shadow Ridge soon."

"I doubt it. This isn't where he lives and works."

Hope sat back down at the table across from her. "You've told me a lot about what happened out there, but nothing really about you and Kellan."

Tess glanced at the door. "Because there's nothing to say."

She hadn't told anybody about her feelings for Kellan, maybe because she didn't know how to talk about something she wasn't sure of herself. Kellan was the unexpected factor that came into her life when she wasn't even looking.

Growing up in a small town hadn't exactly given her a choice of guys to go out with. High school had been more about spending time at the ranch, riding horses, drawing, hanging out with her friends. She'd always figured that she'd meet someone in college, and when college was taken out of the picture, it had left her wondering if she'd ever find anyone. Small-town Shadow Ridge wasn't exactly brimming with eligible men her age, but she'd always felt like she had a lot of time.

Then Kellan had walked into her life.

"Tess?"

She looked back at Hope. "Sorry. My mind was wandering."

"To a certain young man with piercing blue eyes?"

"Stop." Tess frowned. "Even if I did have feelings for him, he lives too far away to make a relationship work, and it's not as if we could have a long-distance relationship. No video calls, no visiting whenever we wanted to. No hanging out. . . That isn't exactly a relationship."

Thinking otherwise was simply going to leave her with a broken heart.

"Love has a way of bridging all the obstacles." Hope's smile faded. "Most of the time anyway."

"We're one step closer to figuring out why the grid went down," Tess said. "Maybe that means you're one step closer to finding Chase."

"I hope so." Hope flicked away an ant crawling across

the table. "Sometimes it's hard to imagine that all this might actually end one day. And that if Chase is still alive, he'll be able to come back to me."

"He's alive. He has to be," Tess said. "And I know he's doing everything he can to get back to Shadow Ridge. Both Chase and Sam."

"I hope so."

Her heart skipped a beat at the knock on the door.

"Kellan's here," she said, forcing herself to stuff down her emotions.

"Are you okay?"

Hope waved away the concern. "Don't worry about me. Every once in a while I just get nostalgic. Go have fun."

Tess slipped outside and shut the door before her sister could invite Kellan in. Maybe it was selfish, but she didn't want to share her limited time with him.

"Hey. . ." Kellan glanced down at the knee-length red and black plaid dress she wore over a pair of leggings, and smiled. "You look beautiful."

"Thanks."

He cocked his head. "Are you okay?"

"Yeah. Everything's perfect."

At least for the moment. Before he left Shadow Ridge.

He offered her his arm, and she took it. This was a moment she wished she could hold on to. Patches of snow laced the yards as they headed toward Main Street. The sky had cleared to stunning cloudless blue, and the air was scented with the hint of cooking fires. But all she saw was the man walking next to her.

"So, what's the big secret?" she asked.

"Have patience." He grinned. "It won't be long."

He was telling her a funny story about an arrest he'd

made last month as they walked down Main Street, when he stopped in front of The Book Nook.

"Why are we stopping here?"

Mr. O'Connor had run the bookstore while his wife taught art lessons in the back studio. Three days after the Quake, his wife had a stroke and passed away a week later. Mr. O'Connor had put plywood on all the windows, securing the property from any would-be thieves. Tess had only seen him twice over the past year.

"Would you like to go inside?" Kellan asked.

"I wish. The Book Nook hasn't been open since the Quake."

"You can't really blame the man. His wife put her heart and soul into that bookstore, and with her gone. . ."

Tess stared up at the crooked sign hanging above them. "She was an amazing artist and teacher, but you sound as if you know him?"

Kellan just smiled. "Maybe we should at least knock and see if Mr. O'Connor is around."

"Kellan, I don't think that's a good idea. He—"

Before she could finish her sentence, the door opened.

"I. . .Mr. O'Connor?" Tess stumbled over her words.

The man had lost quite a bit of weight since she'd seen him last, but other than that, he looked the same with his thin hair, black-framed glasses, and cardigan.

"Why don't the two of you come on in," Mr. O'Conner said, moving aside. "Sorry it's so dark."

Still unsure what was going on, Tess stepped onto the wood floor and into the familiar crowded bookshop that was lit with a few lanterns. The walls were almost completely covered with bookshelves filled primarily with detective magazines, crime novels, time travel sagas, sci-fi, and suspense. Any space left was covered with framed prints. A small chandelier hung from the ceiling, and next to a cozy, red wing chair, there was a wooden ladder to reach the higher shelves.

"How are you, Mr. O'Connor?" Tess asked, not knowing exactly what to say or why they were here.

Everything she'd heard about Mr. O'Conner confirmed his refusal to let anyone in after his wife's death, and that he hadn't changed anything in the shop.

"I'm doing okay," the man said. "Better."

"Long story short," Kellan said, "we just found out that Mr. O'Connor and I are related."

"Related?" Tess asked.

Mr. O'Connor smiled. "My wife was Kellan's mother's cousin."

"We spent a few hours talking yesterday, and it turns out that we also have a lot in common," Kellan said. "Crime books, old cars, and not having family around."

"Wow." Tess looked up at Kellan. "That is not what I was expecting, but that's wonderful."

"Tess McQuaid. You were my wife's favorite student," Mr. O'Connor said. "She told me you had more talent than anyone she'd ever met."

"She was a fabulous teacher. Encouraging. Full of knowledge," Tess said, still trying to figure out why she was here.

"That's why I've changed my mind about something." Mr. O'Connor signaled for them to follow him to the back of the bookstore to the separate, sunlit art studio.

Tess couldn't help but smile as she stepped into the familiar room. It had always been the perfect art studio. For years, Sarah O'Connor had taught her students here.

The lighting was perfect and the space large. To Tess it had been magical. Paintings, art supplies, and art books lined three of the walls. The fourth held a row of floor-to-ceiling windows overlooking a large yard filled with spindly oak trees and Sarah's flower garden. She'd had north-facing windows installed to help regulate the light. Tess had no idea how many hours she'd spent lost here where her mind could go free with her drawings.

"Somehow we got talking about art school and your desire to go back one day," Kellan said.

"I've decided to open up the studio again," Mr. O'Connor said. "It would be a way to remember my Sarah, and I know it's what she would want me to do. I thought. . ." He hesitated. "I thought you might want to give some art lessons. We all need a break from what's going on. In return, you'd have complete access to the studio and supplies."

Tess looked at Kellan then back to Mr. O'Connor. "I don't know what to say."

"I know you have a lot on your plate right now," the older man continued. "You can start small. Maybe by coming here a couple of days a week. Drawing on your own. Painting."

Tess didn't even try to stop the tears. "I couldn't begin to thank you for this."

"I'm the one who will need to thank you if you agree. My wife had a large collection of books for art students. Art history classes, essays, introduction of various techniques, sculpture, and more. I want to open this up to the community. I want to stop hiding. We might not know what the future holds, but we can't forget the past. My wife believed that art and imagination were crucial to life. I don't want to lose that."

Tess reached up and gave the man a big hug. "Thank you."

She didn't miss his smile as he turned to Kellan. "I'll leave the two of you alone to talk."

Kellan turned to her as Mr. O'Connor went back into the bookstore. "It's a bit DIY, but you can go to art school now."

"You did this for me?"

"Yes, but don't look so surprised. I thought you might have noticed how I feel about you. I'm hoping you feel the same way."

"Right now, I'm feeling completely overwhelmed by everything. About the art supplies and this studio. Thank you."

"You're welcome."

"As for my feelings toward you. . ." She smiled up at him. "No, you didn't imagine it."

"Good."

Tess felt her heart pounding in her chest as Kellan took her hand. "I've never been great with words, but this is perfect."

She took a step toward him. Love had come unexpectedly, but now that he was standing in front of her, she couldn't imagine thinking of moving forward with anyone else.

Love?

How could that one word both terrify her and make her feel like she could take on the world as long as he was by her side?

"I've never met anybody quite like you," Tess said.

"Your commitment to your town and the county. Your desire to keep people safe. The way you made me feel safe out there in the desert. And the way you look at me. No one's ever looked at me that way."

"It's because I'm in love with you, Tess McQuaid."

She hesitated, not because she didn't feel the same, but because it seemed so complicated. She didn't want a relationship where they rarely saw each other.

"You're hesitating," he said.

"Not about my feelings toward you. But a long-distance relationship. . . I don't know if that's something I can do. Lose my heart to somebody but not be able to see them."

He squeezed her hands. "What if I lived closer?"

Her brow furrowed. "But you don't."

"What if I worked in Shadow Ridge?"

"With my brothers?"

"The topic might have come up. They could use someone else with experience, and there are several empty houses in town near the police station where I could live. And it would allow you and me to spend more time together. Get to know each other."

"You would do that for me?"

He pulled her hands against his chest. "I would do that for us."

Tess felt her heart melt, followed by a feeling of immense peace.

"So what happens now?" she asked.

"I take your brother up on the offer to move here."

"And the sheriff? Will he understand?"

Kellan nodded. "He has a soft spot when it comes to love. He'll understand."

"There is one more thing I'd like from you," Tess said, still barely able to breathe.

"What is that?"

She wrapped her arms around his neck and smiled. "I would very much like you to kiss me."

CHAPTER TWENTY

TESS GLANCED around the Sunday dinner table, feeling a sense of contentment she hadn't felt for a long time. Her father sat at the head of the table next to Margaret, who had outdone herself with the midday meal of roast, potatoes, carrots, salad, and beets. Hope was here, along with Levi and Ava, and Jace, Morgan, and Noah.

And next to her was Kellan.

"Margaret, this is absolutely delicious," her father said, spooning more potatoes onto his plate and making Margaret blush.

"I don't remember the last time I had a home-cooked meal like this," Kellan said. "Thank you for inviting me."

"You're always welcome," Margaret said. "I heard you were joining the police department here."

"Yes, ma'am, I am."

"He's going to be a great asset," Jace said, "though I think my little sister was in on the decision-making on this one."

This time Tess was the one who felt her cheeks heat as she looked at Kellan.

"I know you're not used to big families," she whispered, "and all of my family isn't even here."

"I'm fine. I feel like I have a family again."

"Speaking of good news, Morgan and I have an announcement to make." Jace wiped his mouth off with his napkin, then scooted his chair back from the table.

Noah sat on the other side of Morgan with a broad smile on his face while he wiggled in his chair, as if he was doing everything in his power not to tell a secret.

"I hope this has something to do with the two of you getting hitched finally," Levi said, glancing at Ava.

Tess waited for the welcome announcement, but wouldn't be surprised if both of her brothers were married in the next few months.

"Morgan," Jace said, "go ahead and tell them."

Morgan took his hand and stood up. "This has been a long time in coming, but we both feel like the timing is right. It doesn't have anything to do with a wedding, though. Jace has been extremely supportive of me and my proposed business venture. I'm going to reopen the café."

A couple of hoots rose from around the table. Tess clapped her hands, catching the adoring look Jace gave Morgan.

"This is going to make the entire town extremely happy," Tess said.

"Agreed," Ava said. "Opening the cafe is going to feel like a step toward normality."

"I think you're both making a great decision," her father said, smiling at the end of the table. "And although

I'm pretty spoiled here with Margaret, I'll be there expecting some of your homemade pie!"

"Morgan always had the best pies and barbecue for miles around," Jace said before kissing her.

Kellan leaned forward. "Maybe that means we can finally have our first official date at a proper restaurant."

Kellan reached under the table and squeezed her hand. So much had changed since they'd gotten lost together in the desert. Kellan had been her hero, but he'd also become someone she couldn't imagine being without.

"There is one other thing." Jace nodded at Noah, who scrambled out of his chair and scurried around until he was standing between Jace and Morgan.

"What's going on?" Morgan asked.

"I would never want to outshine your news, but I had a talk with your son, and he gave me permission to ask you to marry me."

"What?" Morgan pressed her hand against her lips while Jace got down on one knee and held up the diamond solitaire that had been their mother's.

"Morgan, you know I love you with all my heart, and now, I want to ask you if you'll be my wife."

"What do you say, Mom?" Noah asked, pulling on her arm.

"Yes. . ." Tears streamed down Morgan's face as she answered. "Yes, I'll marry you."

"It's about time," Levi said.

"When's the wedding?" Hope asked.

"Morgan and I will have to talk," Jace said, slipping the ring on her finger and holding her gaze, "but as far as I'm concerned, soon. Very soon."

"I have no problem with that," she said, wrapping her arms around Jace's neck and kissing him.

"Yippee!" Noah said.

"I think we need to celebrate," Margaret said, standing up from the table. "I happen to have apple pie for dessert as well as some fresh cream."

"I'll help," Ava said.

Tess squeezed Kellan's hand. "Would you like to step outside on the porch and get some fresh air?"

Kellan nodded and followed her outside. The snow had melted across the desert, framed by a panoramic view of the mountains.

"I'm glad you're here."

He laced his fingers with hers as they took in the view from the veranda. "Me too. I've never had a family like this, and I like your family. A lot."

She beamed up at him. "I'm glad."

"I like you too, you know."

"So no regrets on leaving Van Horn?" she asked.

"How could I have regrets when the reason I'm here is the beautiful woman standing in front of me?" He brushed his lips across hers. "I really do appreciate the way they've made me feel at home. And I have to say, because I think none of you realize it, I think your father's a bit sweet on Margaret."

"What?" Tess took a step back. "I don't think so. She's been a friend of the family for years. She's helped my dad through months of physical therapy, and in a lot of ways has kept our family together. But there's no romance there."

"I'm sorry. I didn't mean to upset you."

"It's okay, it's just that. . ."

Tess glanced back at the house. Maybe she'd missed something she didn't want to see. Somehow, the thought of someone replacing her mother was overwhelming, but if she made her father happy. . .

"I'm sorry," Kellan said, shaking his head. "I never should have said anything. I know you miss your mother, and that no one could ever replace her, but your father. . . I don't know. He seems to light up when she's around."

Had she really missed that?

She had noticed her father smiling more than usual. Maybe there were feelings that he and Margaret didn't even realize. Tess had been excited about Jace finding Morgan, and Levi and Ava, but she never thought about her father falling in love again. And yet he'd been lonely. Losing her mother had put a hole in his heart she hadn't been sure he was going to recover from. Finding that right person. . . She looked up at Kellan.

It really did change everything.

They'd all been affected in one way or another by the past year's events. Dealing with loss might have become a part of daily life, but it also made her appreciate more what she had.

Like today.

Like Kellan.

A rider on horseback came up from the main road that led up to the house. Kellan reached for his sidearm, then moved her behind him.

"Identify yourself," Kellan shouted to the stranger as he dismounted and started walking up to the house.

Tess stared out across the yard, almost not recognizing the man with a full beard and long hair.

"Sam?" she shouted.

"Tess?"

"Kellan, it's my brother. Sam."

Tess tore off the porch, ran to her brother, and jumped into his arms. He smelled of dirt, and musk, and sweat, but she didn't care. He was alive. She pulled him into a big hug and felt his arms wrap around her.

"Boy, I've missed you," Sam said, taking a step back. "Who is that?"

"Kellan Gray. My...friend. He works with Jace and Levi."

Tess stopped. So much had changed, she didn't even know where to begin. How was she supposed to tell him that their mother was gone, that their father was no longer the chief of police. . .

"Who all's here?" he asked.

"A lot's changed, Sam."

"For all of us." He wrapped his arm around her shoulders, but she didn't miss his frown. "That's why I'm here."

ARE you ready for the next book in this riveting series? You're not going to want to miss what happens next.

It's been over a year since Sam McQuaid has been back home to Shadow Ridge, and this time, he's returning with a bounty on his head.

Welcome to Shadow Ridge, where

LONGMIRE meets JERICHO.

IN TODAY'S WORLD, law enforcement agencies across the country rely on forensic tools, DNA testing, and crime labs. **But what if that technology was suddenly no longer available?** No one in the small, west Texas town of Shadow Ridge knows what took down the power grid, or when it's going to be back up, but everyone knows exactly where they were the moment it went down. And now, with no electricity, no internet, and no modern technology, the men and women responsible for keeping the town safe are going to have to **learn how to fight crime all over again.**

AGENTS OF MERCY THRILLERS

USA Today bestselling and award-winning authors Lisa Harris and Lynne Gentry deliver unforgettable and chilling medical thrillers.

Ghost Heart *(Carol Award finalist)*

Port of Origin (Christy-award finalist)

Lethal Outbreak

Death Triangle

FALLOUT SERIES

From USA Today Best-selling author Lisa Harris comes an epic new series where the survival of Shadow Ridge depends on learning how to fight crime all over again. *Welcome to Shadow Ridge, where LONGMIRE meets JERICHO.*

The Last Day

Survival

Hunted

Frequency

Deception

Shattered

Aftermath

SOUTHERN CRIMES

Despite conflicts that arise between them, the Hunt family is close knit, and when it comes to fighting injustice, they stick together and do whatever it takes to stop that injustice.

Dangerous Passage *(Christy-Award winner)*

Fatal Exchange

Hidden Agenda

THE NIKKI BOYD FILES

A string of missing girls that has haunted the public and law enforcement for over a decade. And for Nikki Boyd, the search is personal.

A CBA Best-selling series.

Vendetta *(Christy-Award finalist)*

Missing

Pursued

Vanishing Point

STAND ALONE NOVELS

A Secret to Die For

Deadly Intentions

The Traitor's Pawn

US MARSHAL SERIES

The purpose of the US Marshals is to

apprehend the most dangerous fugitives and assist in high profile investigations.

Because if you run, they will find you.

And US Marshal Madison James is one of the best.

The Escape

The Chase

The Catch

MISSION HOPE

Romance and adventure drive this two-book series where a doctor is forced to race against the clock to expose a modern-day slave trade, and with an rebel uprising in play, a refugee camp faces the breakout of a deadly and infectious disease with nowhere to run.

Blood Ransom (Christy Award Finalist)

Blood Covenant (Best Inspirational Suspense Novel from Romantic Times)

LOVE INSPIRED SUSPENSE

Deadly Safari

Desperate Escape

Taken

Stolen Identity

Desert Secrets

Fatal Cover-Up

Deadly Exchange

No Place to Hide

The O'Callaghan Brothers Series

Sheltered by the Solider

Christmas Witness Pursuit

Hostage Rescue

Christmas Up in Flames

HISTORICAL

An Ocean Away

Sweet Revenge

Sign up for Lisa's newsletter and keep up with her latest news and book releases! Visit www.lisaharriswrites.com

ABOUT THE AUTHOR

LISA HARRIS is a USA Today bestselling author, a Christy Award finalist for *Blood Ransom*, *Vendetta,* and *Port of Origin*, Christy Award winner for Dangerous Passage, and the winner of the Best Inspirational Suspense Novel for 2011 (Blood Covenant) and 2015 (Vendetta) from Romantic Times. She has fifty plus novels and novellas in print.

She and her husband work as missionaries in southern Africa. Lisa loves hanging out with her family, cooking different ethnic dishes, photography, and heading into the African bush on safari. Visit lisaharriswrites.com to learn more.

ACKNOWLEDGMENTS

I hope you enjoyed Tess and Kellan's story. As I've said many times, there is so much that goes on behind the scene to get my books into my readers hands. My amazing editors, Ellen Tarver and Jane Thornton. Amanda Geaney for stepping in as my VA and bringing order and help to all my multi-tasking. My sweet husband whose support is never ending, along with his ability to make me laugh and help me when I'm stuck on a plot issues. My influencer team, you all are always such a huge encouragement. And my readers who have come along with me on this journey. Thank you!

Selected Praise for Lisa Harris

"This whirlwind fast-paced chase will please fans of Terri Blackstock." **Publishers Weekly** on *The Chase*

"An excellent thriller with well-drawn characters, and the suspenseful start to Harris' new U.S. Marshals series, this will please fans of Catherine Coulter and J. T. Ellison's Brit in the FBI series." **Booklist** on *The Escape*

"Lisa Harris never fails to bring an action-packed, adrenaline-filled romantic suspense to her readers." **Interviews & Reviews** on *The Escape*

"The Traitor's Pawn by Lisa Harris is full of action, mystery, and suspense. From the first page to the last, Lisa Harris captured my full attention." **Urban Lit Magazine** on *The Traitor's Pawn*

"Lisa Harris has quickly become one of my favorite romantic suspense writers." **Radiant Lit Blog** on *Missing*

"An exciting, well-crafted tale of romantic suspense from veteran thriller-writer Harris." **Booklist** on *A Secret to Die For*

Award-winning romantic suspense from the heart of Africa!

BLOOD RANSOM: SNEAK PEEK

PROLOGUE

a narrow shaft of sunlight broke through the thick canopy of leaves above Joseph Komboli's short frame and pierced through to the layers of vines that crawled along the forest floor. He trudged past a spiny tree trunk—one of hundreds whose flat crowns reached toward the heavens before disappearing into the cloudless African sky—and smiled as the familiar hum of the forest welcomed him home.

A trickle of moisture dripped down the back of his neck, and he reached up to brush it away, then flicked at a mosquito. The musty smell of rotting leaves and sweet flowers encircled him, a sharp contrast to the stale exhaust fumes of the capital's countless taxis or the stench of hundreds of humans pressed together on the dilapidated cargo boat he'd left at the edge of the river this morning.

Another flying insect buzzed in his ears, its insistent drone drowned out only by the birds chattering in the treetops. He slapped the insect away and dug into the pocket of his worn trousers for a handful of fire-roasted peanuts, still managing to balance the bag that rested atop his head. His mother's sister had packed it for him, ensuring that the journey—by taxi, boat, and now foot— wouldn't leave his belly empty. Once, not too long ago, he had believed no one living in the mountain forests surrounding his village, or perhaps even in all of Africa, could cook *goza* and fish sauce like his mother. But now, having ventured from the dense and sheltering rainforest, he knew she was only one of thousands of women who tirelessly pounded cassava and prepared the thick stew for their families day after day.

Still, his mouth watered at the thought of his mother's cooking. The capital of Bogama might offer running water and electricity for those willing to forfeit a percentage of their minimal salaries, but even the new shirt and camera his uncle had given him as parting gifts weren't enough to lessen his longings for home.

He wrapped the string of the camera around his wrist and felt his heart swell with pride. No other boy in his village owned such a stunning piece. Not that the camera was a frivolous gift. Not at all. His uncle called it an investment in the future. In the city lived a never-ending line of men and women willing to pay a few cents for a color photo. When he returned to Bogama for school, he planned to make enough money to send some home to his family—something that guaranteed plenty of meat and cassava for the evening meal.

Anxious to give his little sister, Aina, one of the sweets tucked safely in his pocket and his mother the bag of sugar he carried, Joseph quickened his steps across the red soil, careful to avoid a low limb swaying under the weight of a monkey.

A cry shattered the relative calm of the forest.

Joseph slowed as the familiar noises of the forest faded into the shouts of human voices. More than likely, the village children had finished collecting water from the river and now played a game of chase or soccer with a homemade ball.

The wind blew across his face, sending a chill down his spine as he neared the thinning trees at the edge of the forest. Another scream split the afternoon like a sharpened machete.

Joseph stopped. These were not the sounds of laughter.

Dropping behind the dense covering of the large leaves, Joseph approached the outskirts of the small village, straining his eyes in an effort to decipher the commotion before him. At first glance everything appeared familiar. Two dozen mud huts with thatched roofs greeted him like an old friend. Tendrils of smoke rose from fires beneath rounded cooking pots that held sauce for evening meals. Brightly colored pieces of fabric fluttered in the breeze as freshly laundered clothes soaked up the warmth of the afternoon sun.

His gaze flickered to a figure emerging from behind one of the grass-thatched huts. Black uniform ... rifle pressed against his shoulder ... Joseph felt his lungs constrict. Another soldier emerged, then another, until there were half a dozen shouting orders at the confused villagers who stumbled onto the open area in front of them. Joseph watched as his best friend Mbona tried to fight back, but his hoe was no match against the rifle butt that struck his head. Mbona fell to the ground.

Ghost Soldiers!

A wave of panic, strong as the mighty Congo River rushing through its narrow tributaries, ripped through Joseph's chest. He gasped for breath, his chest heaving as air refused to fill his lungs. The green forest spun. Gripping the sturdy branch of a tree, he managed to suck in a shallow breath.

He'd heard his uncle speak of the rumored Ghost Soldiers—mercenaries who appeared from nowhere and kidnapped human laborers to work as slaves for the mines. Inhabitants of isolated villages could disappear without a trace and no one would ever know.

Except he'd thought such myths weren't true.

The sight of his little sister told him otherwise. His mind fought to grasp what was happening. Blood trickled down the seven-year-old's forehead as she faltered in front of the soldiers with her hands tied behind her.

No!

Unable to restrain himself, Joseph lunged forward but tripped over a knotty vine and fell. A twig snapped, startling a bird into flight above him.

The soldier turned from his sister and stared into the dense foliage. Joseph lay flat against the ground, his hand clasped over the groan escaping his throat. The soldier hesitated a moment longer, then grabbed his sister's arm and pulled her to join the others.

Choking back a sob, Joseph rose to his knees and dug his fingers into the hard earth. What could he do? Nothing. He was no match for these men. If he didn't remain secluded behind the cover of the forest he too would vanish along with his family.

The haunting sounds of screams mingled with

gunshots. His grandfather fell to the ground and Joseph squeezed his eyes shut, blackness enveloping him. It was then, as he pressed his hand against his pounding chest, that he felt the camera swinging against his wrist. He stared at the silver case. Slowly, he pressed the On button.

This time, the world would know.

With a trembling arm Joseph lifted the camera. Careful to stay within the concealing shade of the forest, he snapped a picture without bothering to aim as his uncle had taught him. He took another photo, and another, and another ... until the cries of his people dissipated on the north side of the clearing as the soldiers led those strong enough to work toward the mountains. The rest—those like his grandfather, too old or too weak to work in the mines—lay motionless against the now bloodstained African soil.

In the remaining silence, the voices of two men drifted across the breeze. English words were foreign to his own people's uneducated ears but had become familiar to Joseph. What he heard now brought a second wave of terror ...

"Only four more days until we are in power ... There is no need to worry ... The president will be taken care of ... I can personally guarantee the support of this district ..."

Joseph zoomed in and took a picture of the two men.

A monkey jumped to the tree above him and started chattering. One of the beefy soldiers jerked around, his attention drawn to the edge of the clearing. Joseph froze as his gaze locked with the man's. Someone shouted.

If they caught him now, no one would ever know what had happened to his family.

Joseph scrambled to his feet as the soldier ran toward

him, but the man was faster. The butt of a rifle struck Joseph's head. He faltered, but as a trickle of blood dripped into his eye, he pictured Aina being led away ... his grandfather murdered in cold blood ...

Ignoring the searing pain, Joseph fought to pull loose from his attacker's grip, kicked at the man's shins. The soldier faltered on the uneven terrain. Clambering to his feet, Joseph ran into the cover of the forest. A rifle fired, and the bullet whizzed past his ear, but he kept moving. With the Ghost Soldier in pursuit, Joseph sprinted as fast as he could through the tangled foliage and prayed that the thick jungle would swallow him.

BLOOD RANSOM: CHAPTER ONE

KASILI OUTDOOR MARKET

Natalie Sinclair fingered the blue-and-yellow fabric that hung neatly folded on a wooden rod among dozens of other brightly colored pieces, barely noticing the plump Mama who stood beside her in hopeful anticipation. Instead she gazed out at the shops that lined the winding, narrow paths of the market, forming an intricate maze the size of a football field. The vendors sold everything from vegetables and live animals to piles of secondhand clothing that had been shipped across the ocean from charities in the States.

Natalie stepped across a puddle and turned to glance beneath the wooden overhang at the stream of people passing by. Even with the weekend over, the outdoor market was crowded with shoppers. Hip-hop style music played in the background, lending a festive feel to the sultry day. But she couldn't shake the uneasy feeling in the pit of her stomach.

Someone was following her.

She quickened her steps and searched for anything that looked out of place. A young man weaved his bicycle through the crowded walkway, forcing those on foot to step aside. A little girl wearing a tattered dress clung to the skirt of her mother, who carried a sleeping infant, secured with a length of material, against her back. An old man with thick glasses shuffled past a shop that sold eggs and sugar, then stopped to examine a pile of spark plugs.

Natalie's sandal stuck in a patch of mud, and she wiggled her foot to pull it out. Perhaps the foreboding sensation was nothing more than the upcoming elections that had her on edge. All American citizens had been warned to stay on high alert due to the volatile political situation. Violence was on the rise. Already a number of joint military-police peacekeeping patrols had been deployed onto the streets, and there were rumors of a curfew.

Not that life in the Republic of Dhambizao was ever considered safe by the embassy, but neither was downtown Portland. It was all a matter of perspective.

And leaving wasn't an option. Not with the hepatitis E outbreak spreading from the city into the surrounding villages. Already, three health zones north of the town of Kasili where she lived were threatened with an outbreak. She'd spent the previous two weeks sharing information about the disease's symptoms with the staff of the local government clinics, as well as conducting awareness campaigns to inform the public on the importance of proper hygiene to prevent an epidemic.

In search of candles for tonight's party, Natalie turned sharply to her left and hurried up the muddy path past wooden tables piled high with leafy greens for stew, bright red tomatoes, and fresh fish. Rows of women sat on wooden stools and fanned their wares to discourage the flies that swarmed around the pungent odor of the morning's catch.

Someone bumped into her from behind, and she pulled her bag closer. Petty theft might be a constant concern, but she knew her escalated fears were out of line. Being the only pale foreigner in a sea of ebony-skinned Africans always caused heads to turn, if not for the novelty, then for the hope that she'd toss them one or two extra coins for their supper.

Her cell phone jingled in her pocket, and she reached to answer it.

"When are you coming back to the office?" Stephen's to-the-point greeting was predictable.

"I'm not. I'm throwing a birthday party for you tonight, remember? You let me off early." A pile of taper candles caught her eye in a shop across the path, and she skirted the edge of a puddle that, thanks to the runoff, was rapidly becoming the size of a small lake.

Stephen groaned. "Patrick's here at the office, and he's asking questions."

She pulled a handful of coins from her pocket to pay for the candles. "Then give him some answers."

"I can't."

Natalie thrust the package the seller had wrapped in newspaper into her bag and frowned. Patrick Seko, the former head of security for the president, now led some sort of specialized task force for the government. Lately, his primary concern seemed to revolve around some demographic research for the Kasili region she'd been compiling for the minister of health, whose office she worked for. Her expertise might be the prevention and control of communicable diseases, but demographics had always interested her. Why her research interested Patrick was a question she'd yet to figure out.

The line crackled. Maybe she'd get out of dealing with Patrick and his insistent questions after all.

"Stephen, you're breaking up."

All she heard was a garbled response. She flipped the phone shut and shoved it back into her pocket. They'd have to finish their conversation at the party.

"Natalie?"

She spun around at the sound of her name. "Rachel, it's good to see you."

Her friend shot her a broad smile. "I'm sorry if I startled you."

Natalie wanted to kick herself for the uncharacteristic agitation that had her looking behind every shadow. "I'm just a bit jumpy today."

"I understand completely." Rachel pushed a handful of thin braids behind her shoulder and smiled. "I think everyone is a bit on edge, even though with the UN's presence the elections are supposed to pass without any major problems. No one has forgotten President Tau's bloody take over."

Natalie had only heard stories from friends about the current president's takeover seventeen years ago. Two elections had taken place since then and were assumed by all to have been rigged. But with increasing pressure from the United States, the European Union, and the African

Union, President Tau had promised a fair election this time no matter the results. And despite random incidences of pre-election violence, even the United Nations was predicting a fair turnover under their supervision—something that, to her mind, remained to be seen.

Natalie took a step back to avoid a group of uniformed students making their way through the market and smiled at her friend. After eighteen months of working together, Rachel had moved back to the capital to take a job with the minister of health, which meant Natalie rarely saw her anymore. Something they both missed. "What are you doing in Kasili?"

"I'm heading back to Bogama tomorrow, but I'm in town because Patrick has been meeting with my parents to work out the *labola*."

"Really? That's wonderful." Her sentiment was genuine, even though she happened to find Patrick overbearing and controlling—as no doubt he would be in deciding on a bride price. She hugged her friend. "When's the wedding ceremony?"

Rachel's white teeth gleamed against her dark skin, but Natalie didn't miss the shadow that crossed her expression. "We're still discussing details with our families, but soon. Very soon."

"Then I'll expect an invitation."

"Of course." Rachel's laugh competed with the buzz of the crowd that filed past them. "And by the way, I don't know if Patrick mentioned it to you, but Stephen invited us to the birthday party you're throwing for him tonight. I hope you don't mind."

"Of course I don't mind." Natalie suppressed a frown. Stephen had invited Patrick to the party? She cleared her throat. "Stephan did just call to tell me Patrick was looking for me, but it had something to do with my demographic reports. Apparently he has more questions."

"Patrick can be a bit ... persistent." Rachel flashed another broad smile, but Natalie caught something else in her eyes she couldn't read. Hesitation? Fear? "I'll tell him to wait until they are compiled. *Then* he can look at them."

Natalie laughed. "Well, you know I'm thrilled you're coming."

She would enjoy catching up with Rachel, and she had already prepared enough food to feed a small army. It was Patrick and his antagonistic political views she dreaded. She'd probably end up spending the whole evening trying to avoid them both.

"I'm looking forward to it as well." Rachel shifted the bag on her shoulder. "But I do need to hurry off. I'm meeting Patrick now. I'll see you tonight."

Natalie watched until her friend disappeared into the crowd, wondering what she'd seen in her friend's gaze. It was probably nothing. Rachel had been right. Her own frayed nerves were simply a reaction of the tension everyone felt. By next week the election would be over and things would be back to normal.

A rooster brushed her legs, and she skirted to the left to avoid stepping on the squawking bird. The owner managed to catch it and mumbled a string of apologies before shoving it back in its cage.

Natalie laughed at the cackling bird, realizing that this was as normal as life was going to get.

Spotting a woman selling spices and baskets of fruit two shops down, she slipped into the tiny stall, determined to enjoy the rest of the day. She had nothing to worry about. Just like the UN predicted, the week would pass without any major incidents. And in the meantime, she had enough on her hands.

She picked up a tiny sack of cloves, held it up to her nose, and took in a deep breath. With the holiday season around the corner, she'd buy some extra. Her mother had sent a care package last week filled with canned pumpkin, chocolate chips, French-fried onions, and marshmallows. This year Natalie planned to invite a few friends over for a real Thanksgiving dinner. Turkey, mashed potatoes, green-bean casserole, pumpkin pie—

Fingers grasped her arm from behind. Natalie screamed and struggled to keep her balance as someone pulled her into the shadows.

Grab your copy today!

"This whirlwind fast-paced chase will please fans of Terri Blackstock."
~Publishers Weekly

"You don't get it.
I HAVE NOTHING TO LOSE.
That plane crash was a
second chance at freedom.
MY WAY OUT."

#TheEscape by Lisa Harris

THE ESCAPE: SNEAK PEEK

Chapter One.

There is a razor-thin edge between justice and revenge, where the two easily blur if left unchecked. Five years after her husband's murder, Madison James was still trying to discover which side of the line she was on—though maybe it didn't matter anymore. Nothing she did was going to bring Luke back.

Her pulse raced as she sprinted the final dozen yards of her morning run, needing the release of endorphins to pick up her mood and get her through the day. At least she had the weather on her side. After weeks of spring rains, typical for the Pacific Northwest, the sun was finally out, showing off blue skies and a stunning view of Mount Rainier in the distance. Spring had also brought with it the bright yellow blooms of the Oregon grape shrubs, planted widely throughout Seattle, along with colorful wild currants.

You couldn't buy that kind of therapy.

Nearing the end of the trail, she slowed down and

grabbed her water bottle out of her waist pack. Seconds later, her sister, Danielle, stopped beside her and leaned over, hands on her thighs, as she caught her breath.

"Not bad for your second week back on the trail," Madison said, capping her bottle and putting it back in her pack. She stretched out one of her calves. "It won't be long before you're back up to your old distances."

"I don't know. I'm starting to think it's going to take more than running three times a week to work off these pounds." Danielle let out a low laugh. "Does chasing a toddler around the house, planning my six-year-old's birthday, hosting our father for a few days, and pacing the floor with a colicky baby count as exercise?"

"That absolutely all counts." Madison stretched the other side. "And as for the extra weight, that baby of yours is worth every pound you gained. Besides, you still look terrific."

Danielle chuckled, pulling out her water bottle and taking a swig. "If this is looking terrific, I can't imagine what a good night's sleep would do."

"You'll get back to your old self in a few weeks."

"That's what Ethan keeps telling me."

Madison stopped stretching and put her hands on her hips.

"Honestly, I don't know how you do it all. You're Superwoman, as far as I'm concerned."

Danielle laughed. "Yep, if you consider changing diapers and making homemade playdough superpowers. You, on the other hand, actually save lives every day."

"You're raising the next generation." Madison caught her sister's gaze. "Never take lightly the importance of being a mom. And you're one of the best."

"How do you always know what to say?" Danielle dropped her water bottle back into its pouch. "But what about you? You haven't mentioned Luke yet today."

Madison frowned. She knew her sister would bring him up eventually. "That was on purpose. Today I'm celebrating your getting back into shape and the stunning weather. I have no intention of spending the day feeling sorry for myself."

Danielle didn't look convinced. "That's fine. Just make sure you're not burying your feelings, Maddie."

"I'm not. Trust me." Madison hesitated, hoping her attempt to sound sincere rang true. "Between grief counseling and support from people like my amazing sister, I'm a different person today. And I should be. It's been five years."

"Despite what they say, time doesn't heal all wounds."

Madison blinked back the memories. Five years ago today, two officers had been waiting for her when she got home to tell her that they were sorry but her husband had been shot and pronounced dead at the scene. They'd never found his killer, and life after that moment had never been the same.

Madison shook her head, blocking out the memories for the moment. She started walking toward the parking lot where they'd left their cars. She'd heard every cliché there was about healing and quickly learned to dismiss most of them. Her healing journey couldn't be wrapped up in a box or mapped out with a formula. Loss changed everything and there was no way around it. There was no road map to follow that led you directly out of the desert.

"Did you go to the gravesite today?" Danielle asked, matching Madison's pace.

"Not yet."

She slowed her pace slightly. Every year on the anniversary of Luke's death, she'd taken flowers to his grave. But for some reason, she hadn't planned to go this year. And she wasn't even sure why. She'd been told how grief tended to evolve. The hours and days after Luke's death had left her paralyzed and barely functioning, until one day, she woke up and realized time had continued on and somehow, so had she. She wasn't done grieving or processing the loss —maybe she never would be completely—but she'd managed to make peace with her new life.

Most days, anyway.

"You know I'm happy to go with you," Danielle said.

"I know, but I'll be fine. I'll go later today."

Danielle had been the protective older sister for as long as she remembered.

Her sister took another sip of her water and stared off into the distance. "Want to head up on the observation deck? The view of Mt. Rainier should be stunning today."

"I need to get back early, but there is something I've been needing to talk to you about."

"Of course."

Madison hesitated, worried she was going to lose her nerve if she didn't tell her sister now. "I've been doing a lot of soul- searching lately, and I feel like there are some things I need to do in order to move on with my life."

"Okay." Danielle cocked her head to the side, hands on her hips. "That's great, though I'm not sure what it means."

Madison hesitated. "I've asked for a transfer."

Danielle took a step back. "Wait a minute. A transfer? To where?"

Madison started walking again. "Just down to the US Marshals district office in Portland. Maybe it sounds crazy, but I've been feeling restless for a while. I think it's time for a fresh start. And I'll be closer to Dad."

"Maddie"—Danielle caught her arm—"you don't have to move away to get a fresh start. And there are plenty of other options besides your moving. The most logical one being that we can move Dad up here. I'll help you look for a place for him like we talked about, and we'll be able to take care of him together—"

Madison shook her head. "He'll never agree to move. You know how stubborn he is, besides—he visits Mama's grave every day. How can we take that away from him? It's his last connection to her."

"He needs to be here. You need to be here."

Madison hesitated, wishing now that she hadn't brought it up. "Even if Daddy wasn't in the equation, I need to do this for me. It's been five years. I need to move on. And for me that means finally selling the house and starting over. I've been dragging my feet for too long."

"I'm all for moving on, but why can't you do that right here? Buy another house in a different suburb, or a loft downtown if you want to be closer to work. Seattle's full of options."

Madison's jaw tensed, but she wasn't ready to back down. "I need to do this. And I need you to support me."

"I get that, but what if I need you here? I know that's selfish, but I want my girls to know their aunt. I want to be able to meet you for lunch when you're free, or go shopping, or—"

"It's a three-hour drive. I can come up for birthdays and holidays and—"

"With all your time off." Danielle shook her head. "I know your intentions are good, but I'd be lucky to get you up here once a year."

"You're wrong." Madison fought back with her own objections. "I'm not running away. I'm just starting over."

Danielle's hands dropped to her sides in defeat. "Just promise me you won't do anything rash."

"I won't. I've just been doing some research."

Danielle glanced at her watch. "I hate to cut things off here, but I really do need to get back home. I didn't know it was so late. Come over for dinner tonight. I'm getting Chinese take-out. We can talk about it more. Besides, you don't need to be alone today. I'm sure the anniversary of Luke's death is part of what's triggered this need to move."

Madison frowned, though her sister's words hit their target. "You know I love you, but I don't need a babysitter."

"Isn't it enough that I love your company?" Danielle asked. "I was going to spend a quiet night at home."

"Maddie—"

"I might be your little sister, but I'm not so little anymore.

Stop worrying. I'm good. I promise. I just need a change. And I need you to support my decision."

"Fine. You know I will, even though I will continue to try and change your mind. We could go house hunting together. In fact, remember that cute house we walked through that's for sale a couple blocks from my house? It would be perfect—"

"Enough." She reached out and squeezed Danielle's hand. "Whatever happens, I promise I'll still come up for the fall marathon, so I can beat you again—"

"What? I beat you by a full minute and a half last year."

Madison shoved her earbuds in her ears and jogged away. "What? I can't hear you."

"I'll see you tomorrow."

She flashed her sister a smile, then sprinted toward the park- ing lot. She breathed in a lungful of air. Memories flickered in the background no matter how much she tried to shove them down.

For her it had been love at first sight. She'd met Luke in the ER when she went in with kidney stones. He was the handsome doctor she couldn't keep her eyes off. Ten months later they married and spent their honeymoon on Vancouver Island, holing up in a private beach house with a view of the ocean. As an ER doc and a police officer, their biggest marital problem had been schedules that always worked against them. They'd fought for the same days off so they could go hiking together. And when they managed to score an extra couple of days, they'd rent a cabin in Lakebay or Greenbank and ditch the world for forty-eight hours.

Their marriage hadn't been perfect, but it had been good because they'd both meant the part about for better or worse. They plowed through rough patches, learned to communicate well, and never went to bed angry. Somehow it had worked.

When they started thinking about having a family, she'd decided that she'd pursue teaching criminal justice instead of chasing down criminals after the first baby was born so she could have a regular schedule and not put her life in danger on a daily basis. And Luke looked for oppor- tunities to work regular hours.

But there'd never been a baby. Instead, in one fatal moment, everything they planned changed forever.

Madison's heart pounded as she ran across the parking lot, trying to outrun the memories. Five years might not be enough time to escape the past, but it was time to try making new memories.

Tomorrow, she was going to call a Realtor.

She was breathing hard when she made it back to her car. She clicked on the fob, then slid into the front seat for the ten- minute drive back to the house she and Luke had bought. It was one of the reasons why she'd decided to move. The starter home had become a labor of love as they'd taken the plunge and moved out of their apartment to become homeowners. A year later, they'd remodeled the kitchen and master bath, finished the basement, and added a wooden deck outside. Everything had seemed perfect. And now, while moving out of state might not fix everything, it felt like the next, needed step of moving forward with life.

Inside the house, she dropped her keys onto the kitchen counter and looked around the room. She'd made a few changes over the years. Fresh paint in the dining room. New pillows on the couch. But it still wasn't enough.

No. She was making the right decision.

She started toward the hallway, then stopped. Something seemed off. The air conditioner clicked on. She reached up to straighten a photo of Mount St. Helens that Luke had taken. She was being paranoid. The doors were locked. No one had followed her home. No one was watching her. It was just her imagination.

She shook off the feeling, walked down to her

bedroom, and froze in the doorway as shock coursed through her.

There. On her comforter was one black rose, just like she'd found every year at her husband's grave on the anniversary of his death. But this time, it was in her room. In her house. Her heart pounded inside her chest. Five years after her husband's death she still had no solid leads on who killed him or who sent the flower every year. If it was the same person, they knew how to stay in the shadows and not get caught. But why? It was the question she'd never been able to answer.

She'd accepted Luke's death and had slowly begun to heal, but this this was different. Whatever started five years ago wasn't over.

The Escape by Lisa Harris © 2020.

Made in the USA
Middletown, DE
07 October 2022